Journal According To John

Journal According To John

Sheryl A. Keen

iUniverse, Inc.
New York Bloomington

Journal According To John

Copyright © 2008 by Sheryl Keen

All rights reserved. No part of this book may be used or reproduced by any means, graphic, electronic, or mechanical, including photocopying, recording, taping or by any information storage retrieval system without the written permission of the publisher except in the case of brief quotations embodied in critical articles and reviews.

This is a work of fiction. All of the characters, names, incidents, organizations, and dialogue in this novel are either the products of the author's imagination or are used fictitiously.

iUniverse books may be ordered through booksellers or by contacting:

iUniverse
1663 Liberty Drive
Bloomington, IN 47403
www.iuniverse.com
1-800-Authors (1-800-288-4677)

Because of the dynamic nature of the Internet, any Web addresses or links contained in this book may have changed since publication and may no longer be valid. The views expressed in this work are solely those of the author and do not necessarily reflect the views of the publisher, and the publisher hereby disclaims any responsibility for them.

ISBN: 978-0-595-52780-9 (pbk)
ISBN: 978-0-595-51541-7 (cloth)
ISBN: 978-0-595-62833-9 (ebk)

Printed in the United States of America

iUniverse rev. date: 11/04/2008

Prologue

1984

When I was six, I watched my mother climb a podium. She wanted to see how one of her pieces of art would look mounted, so she climbed onto the podium herself. That particular work was to be the centrepiece of an exhibition, and when she ascended in its place, she seemed to take up the entire room. She loomed large to my impressionable mind.

"How do I look up here?" She looked down at us, majestically half-akimbo. She didn't have an assistant at the time, but she had people who helped her set up the exhibitions. On this day, an art history master's intern was assisting her.

"Great," he said, circling the podium and craning his neck slightly to look up at her.

"Just *great*?" She threw her bronze hands into the air. "I want this to be showstopping! This is where I want people to linger in awe of this fantastic, edgy piece of creation. This is where I want them to realize that art can be more than they ever imagined. It's about opening up a whole new world. I want drama right here."

"I think it will achieve that." The intern continued to look up, perhaps unsure of what she wanted him to say.

"You *think*." She sighed. Even at the age of six, I knew that tone; I would hear it all my life. It was the one she reserved for the opinions of others whom she did not necessarily trust and for whom she had little regard. She turned slowly on the podium, as if she were on her own axis.

"I am just trying to find the right way that it should be facing. I want this space manipulated to the fullest extent."

I sat on a chair and watched her turning and imagined a willow tree like the ones I saw all over the city. I believed she looked just like one: tall, dark, slender, and flexible.

"I am taller than *Woman Liberated*, but this should do, I think."

She stood still, looking at the piece with a hand on her chin, perhaps considering the height or some other dimension that the rest of us were not privy to. The piece itself was a Sandra Spence. It was a woman made out of a kind of copper material; a book was fashioned into one of her coppery hands. My mother turned suddenly and looked at me.

"What do you think, John?"

My swinging legs were caught off guard and in midair by the question because I had no idea why she was asking *me*. Sometimes when we were at the gallery together, she lost herself in her art objects and the various acts of choosing, positioning, and showing, so much so that I thought I was one of her less favoured pieces, one she often overlooked. Now her undivided gaze was upon me, and it felt magical.

"You *are* that woman." I pointed to the copper. And my mother was exactly that to me—someone to look up to, someone to gaze and strain my neck at, someone who was showstopping.

She laughed, throwing her head back, her throat bare and arched, with the strange, special lights hitting it so that it looked like an elongated stem holding the beautiful fruit that was her head.

"That's my boy." When she said this, my legs started swinging again with added vigour from the approval she had given me.

"Hear that?" she asked the intern, who shook his head. "We have attained perfection—if there is such a thing." I felt warmth coursing through my blood.

She descended, leaving the podium bare of her presence. In her stead, *Woman Liberated* ascended, and I quickly changed my mind about what I had said. The Sandra Spence piece could not match the presence of my mother on that pedestal. It wasn't the fault of Ms. Spence, or a question of her artistic skills, because *nothing* could have had the impressiveness of my mother's bearing—on that stand or anywhere else.

But that was when I was six and went to the gallery regularly with my mother. It was also a time when I looked up to podiums with naiveté.

1 Feb. 2006

I jumped out of my sleep this morning, feeling disoriented. It took a while to recognise my surroundings because as far as I was concerned, I was still in the dream. It was one of those dreams that seemed all too real; I wasn't falling from the sky, but I was being chased, hounded by dead butterflies that had regressed to the pupal stage and that had somehow come alive. They were mere inches from overtaking me, and I was running through tangled vegetation, cutting and scraping my legs and arms before seeing daylight inching itself through the curtained windows.

"Don't muddy the house, John. It's a bitch to clean."

"But what about my cuts and bruises?"

"Well, if you keep trying to run through twisted entanglements, what do you expect? People who try to run through barriers can only get hurt."

I felt breathless, as if I really had been running for my life, and the fact that I was talking to my mother in my dreams could account for the added palpitations. Even though it was minus twenty-eight Celsius outside, I was bathed in sweat. I listened to my ragged breathing and wondered how many times I had had these dreams. Too many to even count, I decided. It was a script: the same words, the same actions, and too many takes.

Haunted into staying in bed, I was frozen in time. Focus on Saturday. Chores, focus, focus, *I told myself over and over. I hated days like this one. My Jeep Liberty would take longer to start and to get warmed up—so much for unparalleled freedom. Everything would be icy and grey; people's faces would reflect the sad weather, and I would be uncomfortably padded up with too much clothes. There was no good day to have this dream, but sunshine and good weather tended to elevate my mood and spirits.* I will have to make myself go out today, if only to keep a part of my sanity intact, *I mused, remembering there would be another Rotary Club meeting at Lakeshore later in the afternoon. We were planning a fundraiser to raise money for a battered women's shelter. There were no battered men, apparently, and hence, no male shelters.* This evening, there's some kind of party; it is Saturday, after all. *But my mind wouldn't concentrate on what I wanted it to; it just kept going back to the dead butterflies. Back to being ten. But really, had I gotten any older than ten? Perhaps I had degenerated, or perhaps I had just not progressed.*

1988. The summer Olympics took place in South Korea, and a famous TV evangelist confessed to sleeping with prostitutes. I was disappointed. People who preached, especially on TV, were placed on such high pedestals that when they fell, they tumbled hard. People wondered if he *could fall like that, then what could happen to the rest of us? But the rest of us never concerned me. The spectators never had to live up to the same expectations as the performers. Spectators watched, and performers showed. My stepfather, Henry, said it meant the guy was only human. The evangelist was on TV every Sunday preaching about sin, and now he was there admitting to sin. That was a big scoop for the news people; the same media who helped build him up helped brought him down. But while that was big news, the most important day that year had to do with my own personal pedestal. It was not a day I would ever forget. It just went to show that no world news can be bigger than a personal dilemma.*

It was my own historical marker, and it marked me for a long time. My mother had remarried within two years of my father's leaving. A man was absolutely necessary, *she had said;* that was the nature of things. Not because she couldn't live without one, but because their presence made some things easier. Henry and I had gone to the supermarket by ourselves one day because my mother said she was not feeling well. I think she was sick from the idea of going to pick up groceries; such chores always made her feel under the weather. The supermarket, especially on a Saturday, was a thorn in her side, one that was especially pricking. It was like there might be some supermarket catastrophe, an epidemic or something, if she went there. We had been there half an hour when my stepfather got a call from a friend with a busted pipe; it had soaked his entire basement. Henry called my mother to tell her he would drop me off and go directly to assist his friend.

I remember parts of that day like poignant scenes clipped from a movie, the heartbreaking parts you can't forget even after the show is long over. On reflection, I thought it was more like one of the installation pieces I had seen at her gallery. I was in a scene where I was both victim and viewer all at once, examining an experimental montage that was very real but which I wanted to be an illusion. I saw her sitting with her sweat-stained back towards me in the rocking chair that was hers, her hands touching bare skin. The rocking chair was an heirloom; my grandmother had received from her mother. My mother did not use it, or so I thought; she cherished it and often said that several generations were in that chair. Now more than that was in it.

The chair was beautifully crafted, and since she was the curator of a gallery, she knew its value and appreciated its artistic and historic aspects. I remembered the old chair creaking, possibly from age, possibly from too much weight, or maybe it was the act being committed in it. Her hard, ebony upper body reminded me of a strong, well-planted tree, and mine wilted under the newfound knowledge of her transgressions. Hers was a nubile body, cast in shadows and lights and as magnificent as a painting one might see in a gallery, but it was a picture I did not need to see, and it would haunt me for a long time.

I must have bolted outside; my feet took me away from the physical scene but not from the mental one. I vomited everything that was in me, and dry retching spells came after there was nothing left. There is a sense of release after throwing up, but on that occasion, I felt only an empty ache. I cried, looking through my tears at the vomit on the brown-green grass, thankful that even in my grief I could still see, as I was sure I would suffer from immediate blindness, a bleakly humourous thought that did little to lessen my pain. Even though I was in the yard, the scene inside the house closed in on me—the scene I had taken part in by seeing her with him. The chair still seemed to be rocking, and it stared at me. In fact, the whole house was a witness that stared me down and challenged me to do something. But what was there for me to do but try to shut my mind down like the switches on a wall, the ones that cut off all the lights?

It was while I was walking on the lawn that I noticed them. They were lying beside my refuse, lifeless with still wings, and that was odd. Everything died eventually, but I had never remembered seeing dead butterflies before. They were scattered all over the lawn, colourful but *somehow not colourful anymore.* What killed them? *I wondered. Maybe they weren't fast enough to escape the mower. But that made no sense because no mowing had taken place recently, and mowing would have torn them into shreds. Maybe the chemicals meant to kill the mosquitoes plaguing the suburbs of Forest Hill had inadvertently killed the butterflies. Somehow the fact that those butterflies would never fly again touched a nerve deep inside me. No more colour, no more dancing flight, and no more gracefulness. I had the feeling I should cry for them, and any other day I might have, but on that day, I felt like my insides had dried up. The water would not fall. Tabby, our cat, crept by my waste disdainfully, as cats do, and then stepped carefully over the dead insects. She rubbed herself alongside my legs and meowed softly. Maybe she knew; maybe she was crying too.*

"Boy, get inside the house," my mother said afterwards. She now wore a white robe, and I couldn't help seeing irony in the colour of purity and wondered why she couldn't have been this modest earlier.

"I don't want to go in there right now."

"You'll see, as you get older, that we don't always get what we want. I want you indoors, and I want you to stop snivelling."

Her hand held a Virginia Slims of the ultra-light version, the ember burning as she sucked on the filter. I wished I had a sieve too, not for tar and nicotine but for other impurities. Virgie, as she loved to refer to her cigarette, was a woman's symbol of emancipation and power. Maybe she was imitating Virgie, using her sexuality for her freedom and empowerment.

"Don't look so aggrieved—nobody's dead. People have needs. Clean yourself up; puking isn't manly, nor is it becoming."

I left the butterflies on their deathbed, brushed past her by the door, and shut myself up in my room. If she could act like it was a normal day, then maybe I should try too. I thought I heard the starting of the strange black Ford Bronco I had seen outside. Ford, tough—the vehicle for men. Black was a good colour for the occasion, dark and shadowy. I hadn't taken a good look at him, and maybe that was for the best. I had rather he were faceless, nameless, and entirely featureless, a phantom in the night that I couldn't identify. I wondered whom I could or should tell, twisting my ten-year-old mind into knots over the question. What would she do if I told? She would probably be angry. Would anybody believe me over a forty year old?

My father had deserted my mother. I couldn't allow Henry to desert her too; I didn't want to break up their marriage. It didn't matter whether anybody believed me or not because I *knew*. I asked myself these questions because I thought she cared, but did she? When she'd come out of the house in her white robe, her attitude hadn't been that of someone who was concerned. I looked in the bathroom mirror and saw my face, and I knew things had changed. The eyes staring back at me were full of the things I'd seen. Whenever my mother wanted to know if I were telling the truth, she would ask me to look at her. Everything was there in the eyes.

When Henry came back later with the groceries, I'd already made my decision not to tell anyone, and I put on the face I wore for the next eighteen years and went downstairs to help him unpack.

The rest of that day, I did everything in a daze, walking as if I were in a dream, not zombielike but like a drunken man who could still find his way home; could still open and close his door, undress, *and go to bed; could still do the routine. At the end of dinner, which I hardly touched, I sneaked into the liquor cabinet when both my mother and Henry were distracted. I chose vodka because, as Henry would say, there was nothing like an Absolut Vodka, absolutely. I wondered what he would say about what I knew. Would he be as nonchalant about her faults as he had been about those of the preacher on the television? Would he think she was just human?*

I don't remember how much I smuggled to my room, but it was enough to make my head swim and the room spin every time I looked up at the ceiling. It was also enough for a vomiting bout in the bathroom and the feeling I was emptying myself of something toxic. It was the first of many similar experiences. Drinking and then throwing up. Drinking, throwing up. It became a routine like a lot of other things, as if I could clean myself by becoming sick.

As the days went by, I felt myself closing in on myself like a snail drawing in its head for protection, or like a plant I had seen in the Caribbean. It was called Shame-me-darling, and when you touched it, it closed itself. Henry finally noticed something was up with me; one day, he asked, "Is there something you'd like to talk to me or your mother about? You used to be so active, talking nonstop, and now you seem so mute, so quiet and always locked up in your room. Are you feeling ill? What's the matter? You used to remind me of a butterfly, always fluttering here, there, and everywhere. Now it seems as if somebody has clipped your wings." Henry had been my father figure ever since my father had moved to another part of Ontario, but I just stared at him blankly, giving away nothing, as motionless as the butterflies on the lawn had been that day.

"Everything's fine," I lied.

"Are you sure?"

My mother interjected, "Henry, don't be so dramatic. He said he was fine. He's probably just reaching that stage where he gets moody, sensitive, and silent."

"But he's only ten, Martha, and you know how ten-year-old boys behave. They're rambunctious; nobody can keep up with them."

"Not all ten-year-old boys are alike."

"Maybe not, but he was a typical one only days ago."

"Things change."

"I guess they change quickly."

Henry asked me again, and I put back on the face I wore to hide my true emotions. I held my cards to my chest, and no one was the wiser.

From that day, I would stare at my mother as if to remind her that I remembered—not that I could have forgotten. She didn't seem to mind; she would just stare right back at me, brazen and shameless and quite off the pedestal I had always put her on. I examined her constantly, especially her hands, long hands, hands made for touching. But then it was her body too—a receptacle for taintedness. At that time, it was just the one man. Later, I would see her actions as those of a woman engaged in what was referred to as the oldest profession.

I saw a video once where there was a car crash, and someone was able to go back in time and avoid the accident. I wished I could do that too. I wished I had never walked through that door. Well, walking through the door that day was one thing, but there were other days—other trucks and other faceless men, always when Henry was out of town. Soon I became an expert on differentiating between Dodges, Chryslers, Fords, GMCs, and just about anything that had *an engine and transported men. I knew the brand, but I couldn't tell the year. I thought perhaps I could make that a hobby, tracing the year, maybe finding out if a particular type was still being made. I would call my scrap book* A History of Cars and SUVs. *Sometimes I glimpsed their hands on the steering wheels, heard the turbo charge of engines powering away from my once-chaste home.*

2 Feb. 2006

I am making my second entry in this journal. I've taken up this activity on the advice of Maya, my cousin and friend who thinks it will be good for me. I strove hard against the idea of catharsis and all that business of cleansing because I don't know what good having my problems written down in hard black and white will do. If anything, this constant writing must be a continuous reminder of the kind of life I have cultivated. I also don't know many men who write in journals, and I don't want to be a pioneer this way. But sometimes friends win, with their constant and insistent badgering, as only they can. Maya could influence cow to buy milk; her powers of persuasion are limitless. At a time when my marriage has dissolved like Andrews Salts in water, dissolving yet fizzing all over the place, the last thing I want to be committed to is making journal entries, especially about issues that are dark and troublesome, issues I placed at the back of my mind long ago, yet which shaped this shell of a thing I've called my life.

Of course, all of this badgering to journal came after a nasty bar brawl, one in which I ended up the worse for wear. I didn't even know what it was about—something senseless, I suppose. I got a split lip, bruised jaw, bloodied nose, and a righteous headache that just went on and on as if I were banging my head against a wall repeatedly. I had to call in sick and ask one of my colleagues to take over my workload because my face was a mess. But that was just a snapshot of the whole muddled picture. I'm a therapist who specializes in behavioural issues. I could just imagine myself sitting at my desk with my injured face, telling people to clean up their own lives, modify their thoughts, and learn new, more appropriate behaviours. I suppose I could use hypocrisy as therapy. Do as I say but not as I do.

I'm only twenty-eight, but my marriage is over, and I feel that its end was as inevitable as death. I suppose that's a bad way to see it, but being in the marriage and knowing all the details as I do, I see it all through my own perspective. They (meaning my family and my friends) all thought it was a marriage made in Eden—but we all know how that story ended: serpent, apple, and damnable, eternal sin. My wife thought she knew best and that she could fix things, as women usually think they can, but as they say, the road to hell is paved with good intentions. The union wasn't hell, but a tormented mind is, and one tormented mind in a union of two is sure to lead to disaster. Poor Debbie had no idea the disaster was set in motion long before she came along.

5 Feb. 2006

It's taking a little getting used to—this prescribed writing. In my job, I write a lot about other people, not about myself. I was reminded to start only when Maya asked about it. Since she had suggested it, she wanted to know how it was going.

"John," she said, escorting me from the bar and from the fight I had found myself in, "you've got to do something." I'm not sure what I'm supposed to be writing about—fact or feeling, but I suppose they are both related.

"Something about what?" I touched a finger to my lips to see whether they felt as fat to the touch as they felt to my mind.

"About this." She waved her hand around. "If you want to fight, maybe you should choose a worthwhile cause."

"Cause? There was no cause. That guy wanted to pick a fight, and he picked the wrong guy."

After the bar, the cold night air brushed against my half-ruined face, and it jolted me a little but not enough to see my follies.

"Actually, he picked the right guy, a guy who has much on his mind, who is easy pickings for trouble of any kind, who has time on his hands and misplaced energy to vent the wrong way."

"I just wanted to get out of the house," I said, still fingering my lips.

"Why did you call me? You know that there are vehicles called taxis—right?" She held onto my arm, leading me to her car.

"I know, that's how I got here. I could have called one, but have you seen my face?"

"Yes, and so much more."

"Cryptic."

I got in the car, and she slammed the door shut. The thud had a sound of inevitability.

"No, it's all very clear."

I was told I was supposed to just write, to let the words fill themselves on the pages. But words don't flow without thoughts, and the process and effort of thinking is the problem because there are things I would rather not think about. Yet they manifest themselves in my dreams. My marriage was shorter than most Hollywood unions, and that in itself constitutes failure, the comparison of something supposedly serious to those empty shells you see on the front pages of magazines on supermarket shelves, placed for the gullible shopper, who is suckered into a last-minute decision to buy one because the solid, black headline about the lives of others is just too sensational to resist.

I must have said "irreconcilable differences" a million times since the divorce. It's a neat answer for all the questions, a neat answer that means nothing. It's an umbrella that holds everything, including lies and half truths.

"Can't you fix whatever's wrong?" my mother had asked.

"No, Mom, it's irreconcilable." She should know. It was her word too, an opaque word that meant nothing to the undiscerning ear. Whoever came up with the term should have received an award for refining the art of avoidance.

Nobody wins in a divorce, but I think Debbie was the big loser. The divorce was quick because I knew people. That was what the Rotary Club was for. Debbie asked for a divorce, and I gave it to her because for once I could actually give her something. She was so sure that once the marriage started, everything would fall into place. I had hoped they would too, but I knew that they would not. Not even pleats fall into place; they have to be ironed and coaxed to lie flat, and sometimes they even have to be starched. That reminded me never to start something where the ingredients for a successful finish were not all present. My ex-wife reminded me of a tragic hero, not unlike Gatsby or Lear, searching for green lights or struggling through darkness to see. The signs were there before we married—the reserve, the coolness—and later Debbie would change that to coldness. But initially, everything was fine, like the way the sea is calm before it erupts in waves of turbulence.

"You must be the most unexcitable man I've ever known, but it's rather refreshing; males can be so reckless and driven with their hormones. They are like the race car drivers you see speeding along at God knows how many kilometres an hour. They crash, of course; the car breaks into a million pieces, and they jump up unharmed. Then they do it again the next week. Reckless."

I smiled knowingly, allowing her to think as she wished. Why would I rock the boat if I didn't have to? Why would I tell her I'd seen some things that made me untrusting of people and detached from them, especially women? I was a Samson who had seen my Delilah, and I needed to get my strength back without self-destructing in the process. I was a rational, intelligent man who knew that not all women were the same, but I had my experiences, and some experiences are like chains around the neck; you either shake them off or get weighted down by it.

"But I know how to bring you to fever pitch," Debbie continued, since I remained reticent.

"That has never happened before," I said.

"It will. It will just as soon as that impenetrable barrier of yours is broken."

I have always left barriers alone, especially ones that seem impenetrable, because it can be a long time before there is a breakthrough, and there is no telling how much blood, sweat, and tears will be in the process. A man can never stop a woman who wants to fix him, though; she has to stop herself when—bloodied and bruised—she runs into enough walls.

6 Feb. 2006

The reluctant writer in me wants to leave the pages blank, but I'm beginning to understand that sometimes, once you start something, it takes on a life of its own. I keep reading again and again the lines I have written to see if there's anything I'll have trouble reading. What else could I do? I've never heard of an edited journal entry. And if I edited it, what would be the purpose of writing this whole thing? Shouldn't I write my feelings as they come—isn't that the cathartic part? If I edit, would I still be truthful to myself?

The apartment is quiet now, especially after the anxiety and gridlock on Highway 427, all that traffic going home. But the gridlock provides a welcome distraction from my thoughts; the condo is silent and crowded with them. I love Etobicoke because it is quiet, but I think I moved here just to get away from the memory of Forest Hill. Home for two, now condominium for one. Debbie is gone, leaving my name with me. She is simply Debbie Wilkins again, the Clarke dropped. That's the beauty of having a hyphenated marriage name: You can drop it like an unfavourable piece of meat in a supermarket freezer.

I met Debbie on campus. I was running to yet another class and bumped into her, scattering her books. It was the best collision I ever had. I immediately stooped, took out my handkerchief, and carefully wiped off her books. Apparently, she was impressed. She took my handkerchief to her home, washed it, and gave it back to me. Who did such a thing in this day and age? I was impressed, too. So we became friends, then lovers, and after I finished university, I asked her to marry me.

I made the proposal at the Royal Ontario Museum, while we stood under the huge dinosaur exhibition. I did not want the clichéd dinner with applause from intrusive bystanders, happy for two complete strangers.

"Let's get extinct together," I had said, thinking about the sheer height and power of a single dinosaur, the millions of years they had roamed the earth, the common fate they had shared. It seemed as good a way as any to describe the size—the towering magnificence—of the love I felt for Debbie at that moment and the way I wanted to share an eternity with her.

"What do you mean?"

I took the ring from my pocket and gave it to her.

"So would you consider going extinct with me? In other words, will you marry me?"

She put her hand over her mouth like the girls you see on TV, the ones who had won Miss World or Miss Universe. She was genuinely near tears.

"Yes," she finally said. It seemed like we embraced for an eternity.

We walked around the exhibition of dinosaurs. They were colossal in stature and dominance, and yet what we had or were about to take on was more immense. Not even those creatures could overpower that feeling.

We passed the *Tyrannosaurus rex*, the stegosaurus, and the triceratops, name after name from time passed. As we wandered in history, Debbie told me she was going to keep her name.

"Is Clarke too ordinary for you?"

"No, I just want to keep my identity. I'll take your name; it's going to be double-barrelled. Don't worry."

I was feeling too heady to be worried. Women added men's name to their last name all the time. But now I know the perils of double-barrelling: Like the namesake gun, the break-off action is there. Hence, Clarke was easy to dispense with.

Debbie said I dropped her long before the divorce; she wasn't even sure if I had taken her up at all. She was right. You have to be in a solid place to take on some things. I hadn't given her or the marriage much consideration. Well, maybe I did. But when you lack capacity, you fail in your abilities. It's like going into a shop to look at clothes, not because you need to buy anything, but because the shop is there and it won't hurt to look. You browse and look at a particular shirt, and the sales clerk tells you the colour suits you. Hell, you buy it because it can't hurt to have too many clothes or too many black shoes. So many of our conversations revolved around this issue.

"John, I'm tired of being here but not here."

"What's that supposed to mean?"

"It means you treat me like a pair of shoes: You may wear me once in a while, but the rest of the time, I am thrown into a dark corner."

"Wow, I am never intelligent enough to figure out these enigmatic statements of yours. It must be the curse of being a man."

"Do you think your pretence of an inferiority complex by virtue of your being a man is helping anybody? This is what happens every single time. I say something, and you falsely stroke my ego by saying how females are so highly intelligent. It's just your twisted way of evading anything more than a superficial conversation. This self-deprecation of yours—what is it about?"

"Self-deprecation? Are you analysing me? If you are, I don't like it. I am not one of your articles that you can examine and interpret to death. All because I can't figure out your shoes and corner analogy."

"Do you want to figure it out? I feel shut out of your life."

"See, this is what I don't understand. I am here. How much more open can I get?"

"Maybe it's a male thing, but I always feel that there are some parts of you that seem to be out of reach."

"Maybe it's not about me or even about men. Maybe two people can never really know each other in the way that they want to."

"That sounds interesting. It may also have some truth to it, but aren't we supposed to try? I will know you as well as you allow me to."

So I had taken home goods I didn't need, just to hang them in the closet, maybe to look at them or wear them once in a while. Well, maybe I needed them, but I couldn't look after them; it takes attention to remember to dry-clean and steam iron. Upkeep takes effort. The problem was that this was a person with wants and needs. Like sexual needs—not just the physical act of it, but feeling like the other person is with you emotionally. For me, sex was sometimes clinical. It was supposed to be good, but at times it was neither good nor bad; it just came with the marriage. The complications came in when the psychological norms, such as emotions and other social factors, were constantly refused to be taken on by me.

"You are so cold and unparticipative," Debbie said, flinging back the sheets and jumping out of bed like a cat on the prowl.

I lay on the bed, watching her with a strange mixture of detachment and anxiety.

"I thought you said you liked me that way." I looked around the room, trying to avoid direct eye contact with her.

"I didn't know you planned to stay that way. It's one thing to be reserved; it's quite another to lie there like a mannequin, without passion or feelings. Things don't get any easier with you; they just get unbelievably harder." She paced and paced.

I wasn't surprised we had found ourselves in this place. She was angry. Her nostrils flared like a horse ridden too long and too hard over rugged terrain. Her words came out in gushes, the way water comes out of a pipe after a long period of cutoff.

"People don't change, Debbie, not even because you want them to. People just don't change."

I repeated it as the repetition would finally make her understand. I stared at the ceiling—because I didn't want to see her. I already pitied her. In hindsight, maybe I pitied myself. I thought I was an emotionally challenged man, and she was just a normal woman wanting a normal marriage. Why couldn't I be the kind of man she wanted? Why couldn't I get over myself and the things that were holding me back?

"Then why the hell did you marry me?" She stopped pacing. Her fists were clenched at her sides as she stood staring down at me, and I looked at the Calvin Klein written around the waist of the panties she was wearing.

I had reduced this sweet-natured woman to the clenching, unclenching ball of fire that stood before me.

"I asked; you accepted." I felt cold, but I had never pretended to warmth, and it was too late for that now.

"I asked; you accepted," she repeated slowly as if she were trying to decipher a code, a puzzled look on her face. I thought she might slap me up close and personal with an open palm or throw the closest thing she could find at my head, but she did not. She was too dignified for that kind of domestic upheaval. The funny thing was—I wanted her to do it, to hurt me like I was hurting her. Maybe if I had blood running down my face into my eyes from a Michael Layne vase, I would have felt better and had a little reprieve from the situation. I wanted shambles of a kind, but we don't always get what we want.

"But what about love? I asked if you loved me, and you said yes. Was that a lie?"

She was still standing over me, looking at me as if she wanted to break my neck.

"I love you as much as I could ever love anyone—that's what I said, and that's what I am still saying. You took that to mean one thing, but I am sure I meant something else."

She sat on the edge of the bed then, her anger spent, looking unhappy and unloved. I preferred her anger. With anger, all I had to do was observe; with unhappiness, I was tempted to participate, or if not that, to feel something.

"What do you mean?"

"It's not about you," I said. "It's about me not having the capacity to give you—or anybody else—what she needs." Just having to give this much explanation had me threading backwards in time.

"But you can give anything you want to give." Her voice sounded like a plea. I wondered if she really believed that. She reached for my hand, as if by making physical contact, everything would be better.

"No, Debbie, after nearly two years, you should know that." I sank further into the pillows, wishing I could go deeper and deeper but not succeeding. I wished she would let my hand go. Her hold on it was hard, when all I wanted to do was sever contact.

"So what do we do?" She released my hand. I was relieved. I thought she knew the answer.

"I think we both know."

That's how it ended, logically, without the usual banging, bloody finale of things broken. No physical shards, just the usual abysmal detachment and longing for something else. Maybe the ending wasn't a good sign because it reflected apathy, whereas the banging and anger said there was interest. She left me then. I didn't cry; men don't cry. The end was coming like a river that was too full; its banks were going to overflow.

8 Feb. 2006

I told Maya only a week ago that it was funny I always had a desire to help improve other people's lives. When we were much younger, she asked me why I wanted a degree in psychology, and that was my answer: I wanted to make people well.

"*So why not a regular doctor, then?*" *she asked.*

That's good too, but I meant well *in terms of head because that's where all the action takes place. Poor brain; poor body.*

I'm supposed to be a creative, intuitive, understanding, and sensitive man; I'm supposed to bring order to chaotic lives, yet in my own life things are out of sync.

Maya tells me things are bound to be out of place. Of course, this is real life. And Maya fixes things the way she wants them. Smoking marijuana in Bible leaves because they are both from God, which I think is subversive and sacrilegious, being the traditional person I am. But whom does it hurt? Certainly not God, and I hear that he/she has a sense of humour. *The herb and the word*—Maya said them together, liking the way they rhymed, like some mad poet who was high. This was the journal instigator who set me on my way to "looking at my daily life and finding what was authentic." Those were her exact words. I should have bolted then.

If it were up to her, this journal would have a name and possibly a verse of poetry. It was my journal, so an ounce of sanity prevailed. There would be no poetry, just broken, personal prose.

"Why didn't you use tobacco paper like a normal person? Was it your aim to finish an entire Bible on weed?" I am always amused by the Maya's antics and the way she seems to get away with everything unscathed.

"I did that *once* as a statement, and now I am officially a Bible burner?"

"I fail to see what statement you were making."

"Well, here's the thing. I just wanted to say that everything is from the same source—God—because the herb and the word are one."

Her lips were pursed in the mischievous smile she wears when she is up to no good. I loved that getting-high part of university life, where the high made us the best intellectuals we thought we could be. I still didn't want to give it up, but we grew up, and the excuse and shield of youth went away.

"They say he—or maybe it's a she—is vengeful, and I would say he or she would have a pretty good cause."

"God, you mean?"

"Yes."

"I don't see why God should be bitter. It's said the word of God is the staff of life, right? It's spiritual food for the body. If I feed my body with both things that God himself gave us, where is the harm in that?"

Her theories were always cemented in some weird but valid fact that couldn't be disputed.

It wasn't surprising that my friend Paul did not give the same advice as Maya.

"So you want to start a journal? I'll help you find a publisher for it when it's done. I know a publishing house down on Charles Street." He laughed as he revelled in his own cynicism. "I see that Maya has started the feminization; no, let's call it what it is, the vaginization of John. John Clarke, the apostle of Maya. Do you still have balls between those two legs of yours, or did you allow your cousin to cut them off? You know you can't be seen with a journal."

"It's not as if it's for show. I don't plan to walk around with it."

"Well, great, because that's not a good accessory for a man. Worse—look at us. Have you ever seen a black man with a journal? You'll see him with a briefcase, a BMW, or a Bible, but not with a scribe pad. We are the trendsetters for style, and that's not style."

"Don't be so cliché and shallow, and stop perpetuating that pigeonhole mentality. It wouldn't be an accessory. You talk as if it would be a fashion statement, but it's a tool, like a knife, a spanner, or a screwdriver, only I'll be using it to have a better understanding of what's happening in my life."

"Rethink the tool. Don't take thinking out of the box so far. They come up with all this paradigm-shift bullshit, so much so that sometimes you think outside the box, and soon you find yourself inside another box or nowhere at all. Change that journal into a little black book. You know what's happening in your life. You and your wife had some problems, whatever those problems were. She's gone, and here you are. Debbie was great; no, I have to be honest—she was a fantastic catch—but she is gone, and there are so many beautiful women in Toronto. Move on with one of them."

"I've tried that, remember?"

I don't know if I tried to move on or just fill the void created by her absence, but I did go down the dating road for a while. Going through the motions to follow a prescribed social process is just wasteful. Not only is it a pain to get to know someone new, but I found it was even more painful because I wasn't interested. My interest resided with only one person.

"Maybe you didn't try with the right girl."

"I have, and now she's gone."

"Well, that's it right there—she's not here, and a journal will not get her back."

"I want to understand why whatever happened happened."

"God, ever since you and Debbie split, you have become so searching for understanding and truths and what not. You are like a different person. Do you know those people who are always searching for the meaning of life and whatnot? None of them ever found out the answer, and the question is still there. That tells me we aren't meant to know every single thing. We should just enjoy what is presented to us. The whys are not important. You know what *is*; just deal with that. It's not necessary to understand. You can't understand women anyway. They are like puzzles, meant to bend men's minds. Why make our lives more complicated than they need to be? Sometimes you just have to accept the way things are and move on."

"One, it's not solely about trying to understand women; I am trying to understand myself. Two, I am not trying to solve life's deepest questions, just my own. How can I move on if I don't address what went wrong? Aren't I going to make the same mistakes?"

"Mistakes happen, and sometimes we make them over and over again with the same miserable results. Repetition is not necessarily a bad thing. You learn eventually. It's like failure is not really losing. It's just a step-by-step process to winning. You are too in touch with your feelings. You need to play some video games or kick some ball, something that will leave your mind blank and free of all the questions you're juggling inside that head of yours."

My mind being blank would be a sort of paradise, but that would never happen. The conversation with Paul bordered on heavy, and I wasn't sure I wanted to pursue it further. I might let things slip, and I didn't want to. It wasn't the sort of conversation men had anyway. Men see things differently. Paul would never write in a journal, but although he didn't like Maya's logging idea, we both share a love and admiration for her. She told us recently, after breaking up with her boyfriend, that she would be taking a siesta from men. The last straw had come when the boyfriend embarrassed her at work because he wanted her to leave at a specific time. Well, that was it, she said. We admired that about her too, the power and the authority she exerted over her own affairs. I don't know if there's a female equivalent to being gelded, but when it comes to Maya, she's no gelding, that's for sure.

We lived vicariously through the telling of that one Bible-leaf saga. Who else could have come up with that preposterous smoking idea? With anybody else, it would have been just plain stupid, but with her, it was avant-garde. I was somewhere in the middle, smoking herb but not graduating to smoking it in pages of the Bible. With me, that would never happen. I felt that even though Maya got away with it, God would not allow me to; I would be made an example of, and the wages of my sins would be death.

But Maya is persuasive about the journal idea, so there has to be something to it. But then, she could sell anything. Since life is bound to have some things out of place, maybe the act of writing will provide some order. She used the word *self-discovery*. Is that something we do? We are males, already discovered.

10 Feb. 2006

Whenever I take up the journal, I inevitably start writing about Debbie. I get nausea sometimes from thinking about the divorce, and I'm already sick of writing about it. Maybe I have a weak stomach; if it were stronger, I would probably have no need for this journal. I should never have taken up this in-your-face, black-and-white confirmation of my shortcomings. Yet I persist, maybe because the marriage brought up things partially unapproached, things partially hidden. It represents a summary of my life.

Directly after a divorce, all one can do is reflect. Divorce looks like a sort of death. June 2003–April 2005, a headstone of failure. After death, sometimes things that have been hidden come to life, or they get buried eternally. I wonder what will become of my cobwebs. Debbie told me that I hide things I shouldn't. A pattern of hiding, she called it, and everything becomes a pattern if you do it long enough. She discovered one of my bank statements by accident, an account she had no idea I had.

"Why didn't I know about this account?" She sounded as if she were accusing me of something; in turn, I became defensive and annoyed.

"It's my account, nothing for you to worry about. Can't a man have some privacy without all this interrogation?" I was searching for a soft answer but found none, so I went with what was already on the tip of my tongue. Where were the control and the behaviour alteration that I repeatedly asked others to exhibit?

"Is that your answer? Is this a marriage, or is it just two people living together? Are we just roommates who find things out accidentally, if at all? You have your life partitioned off in cubicles, and nobody gets in some sections." I had just come in from work, making it only to the living room, and she was home early from her job at the newspaper.

"Debbie, there is no need to be hysterical." I sighed.

"Hysterical! You stand there and say I'm hysterical, when you know that I constantly have to put up with all this secrecy and covert dealings. You seem to have these operations that must be done like expert manoeuvrings. It's like I'm living with James Bond. You go to places you haven't been, see people you've never seen. What's the matter with you?" She was breathing hard, so I knew that she was mad.

"Nothing is the matter with me; you're just being dramatic." I laughed at the time, but I knew she wasn't just being dramatic. Still, I had to control the situation somehow, and that was a way. If I said she was hysterical, maybe she would associate it with disorder and would quiet down. Debbie didn't like disorder. The house was always neat: the drapes matched the wall paint, the vases were bought in matching pairs, the décor and ambience were just right. Maybe it was a function of her journalistic experiences and tasks: Everything had to be structured the right way for a story's slant, paragraph by paragraph.

I knew what she was referring to. I went to shows and the casino in Niagara Falls with friends when she went to New York to visit her mother. On her return, when she enquired what I had done with my time, I told her nothing. Or I would entertain people whom I would tell her I hadn't seen in a while. She would ask me why all the secrecy, but I couldn't explain. Secrecy was like a stained, dirty carpet; it didn't beautify anymore; it only gathered more and more dust. It made everything ugly, including anything of value in the home, like squatters moving in and depreciating the neighbourhood. The only solution was to root it out and destroy it. But was it secrecy or silence? Whichever it was, I became the very thing I resisted. And in that way, I became tied to the very person I wanted to let go.

14 Feb. 2006

The radio, newspapers, and television stations don't allow anybody to forget that it's the season for valentines. From the organized giants of the Eaton Centre, Yorkdale Mall, and Yorkville; to the man selling roses and flowers on the street, I feel surrounded, like I'm in a hostage situation. This is the time when people profess their undying love for a day. If I had forgotten what day it was, all the women wearing red and white at work would have reminded me, and the ever-flowing bouquets with their suffocating pollen and the boxes of chocolates intruding on the workday kept me informed.

I've given my share of flora, stuffed fauna, sweets, and trips outside Toronto to celebrate. I've often wondered what I was celebrating. Valentines suggest an intimacy and closeness that I have not yet achieved, not the way I want to.

My stepfather owned a plumbing company, and although he could afford to stay home for some jobs, he was a hands-on sort of guy and went wherever the job was, whenever it was. Even Valentine's Day sometimes found him out of town. I'm not sure how or why my mother married Henry, as she claimed she couldn't stand the working man's hand. It lacked the finesse she imagined, not only in the physical but also in the mental realm. She did anyway.

This particular Valentine's Day, he had to be in Barrie, and of course, that was fine with my mother; she was sentimental about nothing that I knew of. I wondered how Henry could stand it. Did her physical beauty make up for her other deficiencies and blemishes? I came home from school, cautious as I became since the first time.

Immediately the hair on my skin stood up. The smell of tobacco pervaded the air, and it wasn't the Virginia Slims kind my mother smoked. It smelled the way I imagined Cuba would smell because of everything I had heard about their tobacco. Standing in the living room, I was at a crossroads—to go back through the door quietly or to creep upstairs to my room.

The cat rubbed itself against the settee with a humped back; the soft rustle of its body against the furniture alerted me to its presence. And there, sitting in the ashtray beside a half-finished Virginia Slims, was the fat, thick, strange, and offending cigar. It looked like it had barely been smoked, but the end was burned, so I knew it had been lit. I could imagine plumes of smoke coming from that large cigar; I could see it covering the entire sitting room in a sort of triumph. All that I felt was utter defeat.

Up the stairs I crept, socks on carpet, trying to walk as stealthily as Tabby with only the slightest amount of sole on ground. He had to have seen me before I saw him; I had my head down to look where I put each foot. I realized there was a strange man coming down the stairs, towering above me like God descending from sky, his large, stodgy, hands holding the banister. I adjusted my eyes so only his profile would take up the edge of my vision. When we passed each other, he seemed to pause. "Hey, Kid," he said. I rushed up the stairs, anxious to get away from his greetings, the words from the strange man inside what was now my not-so-secure home. He smelled musky, like the liquid Henry splashed on his face after shaving. But there was something else, something that reminded me of the odours in the animal cages at the Scarborough Zoo, a crackling air of fear and excitement caused by the prowling, the deep growls, and the knowledge that I could be close to death if an enclosure became open.

"Hey, kid." Those two words had weight. He walked down the stairs as if he owned them, and by extension as if he had power over me. And where was she? Lying in her matrimonial bed, basking in sin, with me feeling like I could walk in there and pound a little chastity into her. This *was why she had hired an assistant curator. The gallery didn't need additional management. It wasn't the National Gallery, just a place where scrap metal reigned. She just needed more time for the erotic pollution that contaminated the entire house and my entire life.*

My footsteps pounding up the stairs, the sound of me escaping from cigar man, must have taken her out of the corrupted aftermath she basked in. When I heard her downstairs, I went down too, and all we did was stare at each other wordlessly. I was angry and ignited, and she was incomprehensible, as she usually was. It angered me even more that she could be so composed and obscure while I was in turmoil. It really pushed me over the edge.

"What in God's name are you staring at?"

I remained speechless, not trusting myself to open my mouth. She paced the sitting room with a cigarette between her long, elegant fingers. She was searching, I guessed by the frantic darting of her eyes, for her misplaced lighter. The ashtray still held the two incompletes.

"Instead of staring at me, perhaps you want to help me find a light." *She stood, arms akimbo, as if she were waiting for me to move. Perhaps her physical stance was a dare; her two pointed elbows did not make me want to compromise. All I saw was an invitation to duel. She was an archer with a bow pointed straight at me. I lurched forward before her, blind with rage, but I only grabbed and hurled the offending ashtray and its content out of my sight. It crashed against one of the walls, leaving a slight grey mark of dust, ending in a sharp clang on the hardwood floor. The cigar and her cigarette landed somewhere I couldn't see them. By the time I knew what I had done, she was on me.*

She was breathing so hard, I felt it like wind on my face. Her hands trembled, but they were still strong enough to collar me up, practically lifting me off the floor. The cigarette she had wanted to light lay broken and trampled under her feet.

"I could slap you silly right now. Are you mad?" Her spittle sprayed my cheek. I was trembling too. I just wanted her hands and body away from me. The grey mark on the wall was shaped like two wings, and it made me think that perhaps I just wanted to be transported out of there.

"Don't touch me," I managed to say.

"I'm using all my willpower not to shake some sense into you."

"Violence is only another disorder, like so many things here."

I heard that said once at school, when they talked about bullying, teasing, and school violence. They said that disorder was like a disease, one causing abnormality in the body and the mind.

She dropped one hand, but I was still pinned in a tight bunch by the other. She used the free hand to grasp my face, bunching the flesh of my cheek against my teeth.

"How dare you? I am your mother, and you will treat me as such. Your disregard for me will not be tolerated." My face hurt, but I still managed a laugh. I wanted to tell her that she was just a whore and not my mother as she insisted, but I couldn't because once I crossed

that line, there would be no going back. If I said it out loud, that would give it weight and make it true. From that, there would be no recovery.

"Oh, right," I said. "Happy Valentine's Day, Mother. I wanted to say that when I came in, but you were occupied."

She let go of my face, and my head snapped backwards. She pulled me closer towards her face until our noses touched. Her breath became my breath, and maybe mine was hers too.

"Do you take me for a joke?"

"No, you do that all on your own."

"Don't wear bigger briefs than you have a dick to put into them. I'm warning you: I have had enough of your tantrums. Just grow up."

"Just let me go."

She released me from the mixture of Chanel, tobacco, and sex that was her.

"Go clean up that mess." She waved a hand in the general direction of the ashtray, took a new cigarette from the box, and started in search of a light again. Nothing changed; it was simply "as you were" before. I turned towards the stairs.

"Come back here. I told you to clean up this mess."

"It's your mess." I headed up again and left her standing there.

When I came down for dinner, the wing-shaped spot on the wall was gone, blown away as if it had never been there, and the ashtray had been replaced. Henry would be spending the night in Barrie, so it would just be the two of us. She must have timed her rendezvous around his schedules, and I don't know how he didn't pick up on the fact that something wasn't right. I toyed with the idea of deliberately *doing something to force him to change his plans, but I gave up the thought just as quickly as it came to me. I took out the chair at the place I was going to sit, but she stopped me.*

"I want you sitting beside me this evening." She patted the seat beside her in coerced invitation.

"This is where I usually sit." I was still drawing out the same chair.

"Yes," she said, "but I want you right here beside your mother." She had a smile on her face, but I heard steel in her voice. I sat where she wanted me to. There wasn't much fight left in me. I had to save some for the next time—like they say, living to fight another day. She took tongs and served me tomatoes, broccoli, cauliflower, and cucumbers. It seemed like overkill; although I didn't hate vegetables, I didn't know why she wanted to give me so much.

"I can serve myself."

"But I want to. Besides, these are good for you, and you want me to be good to you, don't you?"

I didn't answer her. I didn't know how the goodness of vegetables matched up to the goodness of her. She placed her hand on my chair, allowing her hand to fall somewhere along my shoulder.

"Why can't you be good to me too, uh? John, I had to clean up your mess this evening. Is that what you want to do—create work and anxiety for me? Why don't you cut your mother some slack? I have my desires, and you are not going to stand in the way of them. Do you understand what I am saying?" Her hand caressed the line of my jaw as she spoke. She wasn't eating, just watching me while she had her monologue. "I provide you with a good home, good school, and more

than the basic amenities of life. I give you space and freedom. Why can't I get some of that from you too? Please reciprocate."

I brushed her hand away from my face, but she put it back, deliberately, as if to annoy me.

"I want you to be a good boy, eat your vegetables, and think about allowing me to exercise my free will." She laughed. "I used the word allow *as if you are responsible for me. Do you see how you have reduced me to an immature way of thinking? Do you see how you have reduced me to asking permission from you? Well, I want all this to stop. You are the son, and I am the mother.* I *have control.*"

She had talked herself out. She left the table without touching a bite. I heard the sliding of the wheel on the lighter and smelled the burning of Virgie.

I just sat, ate the vegetables, and thought about wholesomeness.

Debbie and I had rituals before we were even married. If Valentine's Day fell on a weekday, we would go somewhere on the weekend. Usually we went to Niagara because of the convenience, or to Quebec if we really wanted to go further. Quebec was great, with its distinct, European feel and Winter Carnival, but it wasn't our favourite place because of our lack of fluency in French. The language challenge often took something away from the trip. I loved to drive, and Debbie loved the long drives. She said there was so much beauty and a sense of expectancy, maybe an expectancy that this time around, things would be different, but they never were. Once we arrived at whatever hotel it was, I would get the sense that the best part of the trip was over, and then a desperate sense of melancholy would set in. The best thing about these hotels was that the liquor was always flowing. Everything became better looking with alcohol, past, present, and future. All things were possible when your senses were dulled.

Debbie didn't like it when I drank. According to her, I would drown myself in the stuff or was trying to drown something else. My response was to laugh and ask her why I would possibly want to do that. She would always sense something; I guessed that was her intuition. But she didn't know what, that's for sure, and a lack of knowledge isn't always bliss. Our last Valentine's Day weekend didn't end as Cupid had intended. The nudity was there, but the arrow was in all the wrong places. We arrived on Friday night; she wanted to sleep in on Saturday morning. I wanted to do anything but that. We were in one of those rooms where you could see the rustic beauty of the area. It was winter, but there was no mistaking the charm and quaintness of the place.

"Why don't we stay in bed? We can get up for lunch." She reached to pull me back down from my sitting position, but I remained firm.

"I don't feel like it."

"Well, here's a first. You can actually *feel* something, which makes you human. Why is it you don't want to get close to me? That's what this is all about, isn't it?" She lowered herself back into the bed after seeing I wouldn't budge.

"Don't be ridiculous. I just want to see the surroundings."

"Time enough after lunch. It's not as if you haven't already seen the clock tower, that old medical place, and the church before. You could practically give a tour of the place, the number of times you have seen it. John, if you want this marriage to work, you've got to compromise. You don't want to get close to me;

when we make love, you either lie there like a mannequin, or you rush through it like it's a race you want to be over."

All the time she was talking, I looked out through the patio, listening to the scraping sounds of someone clearing the light snow that had fallen. Always pushing, pushing and grating, gathering momentum and weight, and finally, the dash into a waiting lump of snow.

"It's called an apothecary."

"What?"

"That place you called the old medical place. That's what it's called. In colonial days, that's where they performed surgery, handed out prescriptions, and even gave lessons to midwives. Apothecaries often operated through retail shops, and in addition to ingredients for medicines, they would also sell tobacco."

"That's quite fascinating and interesting—and I might even store it in some part of my memory in case I need that historical info in the future—but that's not my focus right now."

She exhaled slowly, as if to let out some pent-up emotions, and then she smiled and touched my arm.

"Just touch me, and I'll touch you, and not just your physical hand. All you have to do is place your hands on me and allow me put mine on you." She released the sarcasm and attempted to get close.

I gave in that time, not because I wanted to compromise but because she was always the one who compromised, and I knew that sometimes I would have to give in. So I forced myself to lie back on the bed and do what normal couples do in a hotel room on Valentine's Day weekend.

Saturday night before dinner, at dinner, and after dinner, I drank more screwdrivers than I could count because whatever the night required could be done a lot easier with spirits. Sunday morning before checkout, I spent most of the time ejecting all the liquid I had consumed the night before. While my body rejected what it did not want, I thought, *I don't like to be touched. I don't like to be touched. I feel helpless. I feel helpless.* This was a déjà vu of eighteen years ago. But what was it about touching that I did not like? They didn't touch *me*; they touched my mother, and seeing her with them made me feel vulnerable and powerless. Being with the woman I loved brought those same feelings. In a strange way, a lot of transference took place, and here I was with them, just grasping after a little control.

18 Feb. 2006

My last entry shook me a little, taking me from a sort of numbness to a sort of tingling stage, like muscles that become unfeeling after sitting in a cramped space for too long. There's a tingling sensation before the blood starts to circulate and everything becomes normal again. It's strange how big things can be compressed and tucked away in a compartment of the brain where you don't want to find them, but if there's just a slight shift, everything comes tumbling down.

Although I had a good relationship with my father when I was younger, I've always felt a little betrayed by him. When I was seven, he and my mother separated; they both sat me down and told me the usual story: They loved me and would always love me, but they couldn't live together anymore. The last time I saw my father in our house, he tried to hug me good-bye, and I remember clearly how I shouted, "Don't touch me!" After he left, I cried and cried, feeling disabled all the while. It was near summer, and my mother promised to take me to Vancouver for the holidays. I knew she was trying to make up for the loss. We went, and I remember going to the Vancouver Aquarium near Stanley Park, where my main interest was the butterfly collection. When I saw the different species with their brightly coloured wings and their constant restlessness, I felt my life wasn't so bad after all, and as my mother said, things could have been worse. The people at the Aquarium spoke passionately about our personal connections with the butterfly and how we could support conservation efforts at home. They gave everybody a butterfly garden-seed mix.

The day filled with butterflies was the highlight of my holidays. Years later, I learnt about the citrus swallowtail butterfly and the monarch in high school, and I remembered that trip to Vancouver. I especially loved to hear about the monarchs because they are capable of long-distance flight. Once, I stood in the yard and saw them flitting around with all their gay colours. I used to watch the cat watch the butterflies. It was really my mother's cat; she said she preferred cats to dogs because cats took what they needed and then went back to themselves. Dogs, apparently, were too needy and clingy. Why didn't she understand that they were loyal too? The cat would crouch very still, biding its time, and then it would pounce, trying to catch one with its well-honed claws. But the cat never did land a butterfly; they were much too quick. My associations with butterflies are not of Vancouver anymore. I still remember that holiday, but I also remember something else—or rather, I try to forget something else.

There is a cruel twist in the process of trying to forget: You always seem to remember. If you repress a memory in order to cope, it somehow backfires on you. It's like spitting through the window of a speeding car on a windy day; it slaps you right back in the face. Butterflies could be the symbol of light, life, hopes, and dreams, but I find they can also represent fantasy and despair. The one thing I know about symbols is that it is our experience that shapes the reality of them.

When I was thirteen, and shortly after that Valentine's Day experience, we had to write a poem and recite it in class, and we had to critique the work of our peers. A boy in my class wrote a poem about the colours of the butterflies; the colours represented love, peace, and hope. When it was my turn to critique, I said, "The poem is null and void. Butterflies don't represent anything; they are just entities unto themselves, like stones or trees or whatever. I don't see any hope or love when I see a butterfly. I just see an insect that looks like a moth. It has four wings, and it's more often seen in warm months, flying around sucking nectar from whatever flowers it can find." I surprised myself with how violently I said all that, and it seemed I surprised my classmates also because everybody looked at me as if I had gone insane.

Surprisingly, my poem was about butterflies too, and if I try hard enough, I know that I can remember exactly what it said, but for now, I don't think I want to. Sometimes what's tucked away in the compartment doesn't just tumble out; sometimes it gradually unravels with the shift or is plucked out without warning.

20 Feb. 2006

Last night we went to the True Words café on Spadina to take in a blend of live reggae music, poetry, and dub poetry. We ended up in a pleasant argument, like so many others that we have. One of the dub poets, who goes by the name of Blending Strawberries, was mouthing off about lost love. She rapped away about stolen lands.

"You took my land
I never understand
You had your own plans
But now I know I'm on sinking sand."

The usual rhyming lines resonated throughout the café, and the usual disgust reverberated through my head.

"Why do females always write and sing about being left torn and broken, as if they have no control over their own lives?" I already had a good buzz from the screwdrivers I'd been drinking. I had a good five, compared to Paul's two. Maya was having the usual one glass of red wine, which she would nurse all night.

"Personally, I don't mind hearing it as long as I don't have to hear about it all night. But it's her first poem—give it a chance, John." Maya looked at her face using a small mirror and put a little powder here and there as she spoke. She snapped it shut and replaced it in her bag when she finished talking.

"John, is there something wrong with you? Don't you know that once a female gets a platform, she will use the opportunity to dog us out? You say to them, 'Here's a podium. What's your manifesto?' And they say, 'Men.'" Paul turned to look at me as he said this.

"I don't know about that; I just can't sit through the kind of drama that some women seem to love. The best part is that they do have control, and they use it however they want to. Christ, to listen to them, you would think we still rule the world with dick in hand."

"First of all, you still do—rule the world that is. Whether it is with a dick or a big stick, I don't know, but it's all the same—something phallic and threatening. Secondly, Paul, I take offence to the nonsense that comes from your mouth. Not all of us are alike. Do you see me beating up on you guys?"

"You're different—almost one of the boys."

"Gee, I am so flattered."

"That's a compliment, I'll have you know."

"Plus, who knows what you and your girlfriends talk about when we're not around?"

"You can rest assured, you are never a topic."

"What about your ex—is he a topic?"

"And why shouldn't he be? He's a prime example of the kind of men women should run far away from, the control freaks who tell you what to eat, when to sleep, and even when to breathe."

It went back and forth from there, with Maya saying people should be allowed to express themselves and me saying I agreed but that people should just move on and stop playing the victim card, which was all an act anyway. Sometimes there were things that could have no middle ground, but maybe I was just an extremist. I know I don't have problems with other people's emotions; I just have problems with my own. Maybe they are interrelated, or maybe my own problems projected themselves to others around me.

Why should I care so much if people want to sing about breathing again, can't live without you, or are lost in love? They feel. They sing. You bottle things up, you explode or slowly die inside. I don't know which I'll eventually end up doing, but I feel it's all coming to a head.

23 Feb. 2006

The days are racing towards—what, I do not know. Today at work I was told I'd be given additional responsibilities. I will be dealing with substance abuse issues, in addition to the everyday relationship issues. My case load was already overwhelming, but I still welcome the additional diversion. I'll be moving from the Social Board to the Department of Mental Health on Albert Street, in the heart of downtown. How much more would I have accomplished if I'd pursued my master's degree? I don't know if I need it. It's possible my first degree, hard work, and dedication will carry me through. I'll start my new position in a couple of weeks. I received the news graciously enough, I think, and I accepted the congratulations as best as I could. Yet the sense of elation I should be feeling isn't there. I have no fear of moving to this new position and the new physical space. For a long time, I've attached myself to nothing, so severing is easy.

It's a move I think I deserve. All I have is my work, and that's what I put my all into. My mother and my aunt think I should still be married to Debbie and that I should be putting my time into making a family. I could understand my aunt wanting that; she's been married to the same man for over thirty years. If she claimed to be an expert in all things marital, I would believe her. But my mother is a puzzle I can never figure out. She should still be married to my father—or to Henry—but there she is, single again. Maybe that's best for everyone. Every time they talk about me not getting any younger, I tell them that nobody is. It's not as if I have a biological clock; nothing is ticking away within me. Females talk about the race against time, but I maintain that sperm is good to a ripe old age. If it isn't, then maybe reproduction is just not meant to be. More and more I feel that I am racing with myself, so only I can win or lose.

Neither my mother nor my aunt seem to know about my silent duel with myself, and how long and quiet a shadow it has cast on eighteen years of my life. It's strange how it all seems like yesterday, but I count it repeatedly, and it actually has been eighteen years. That's almost two decades! Every time I count the years, I feel like I'm ten all over again, and I wonder if there ever is an age of innocence. Maybe it's the years before ten. Is there really an age of innocence, or are we all exposed to the rabid claws of life too soon? Maybe a decade of innocence is enough, but when should one move from an innocuous existence to that other form, the one where light becomes dark, day becomes night, and all that one thought was good becomes tainted?

Some things, when tainted, become hard to make clean again. Sometimes the tainted becomes an all-invasive corruption that needs a strong cleaning portion. I've often wondered what would be strong enough for me.

25 Feb. 2006

I picked up one of those *Writer's Digest* magazines, an issue that talks about journaling. I finished lunch early and decided to pop into Bookland to see if there were any interesting books or magazines, and lo and behold, there it was, with "Personal Journaling" in bold letters, as if it were speaking to me personally. Normally I wouldn't even see these kinds of magazines, and so I wouldn't have noticed such a headline. After all, these are female, Oprah-like domains, but thanks to Maya, the word *journal* is firmly planted in my head. I bought it, bagged it, and slipped it into my briefcase for later.

I can't remember the name of the person who wrote the article that I read, but I'm sure the author must have been a woman. After all, how many men give other men advice about keeping a journal? Well, she said that journaling can help one pursue self-inquiry, develop compassion for oneself, and basically show one how to live fully. Hell, if the seemingly meaningless dribble I write daily can help me acquire all of the above, then I'll write every day, God forbid. I do feel as if I'm trapped in time. I've been asking myself questions for years, but perhaps I'm inquiring along the wrong lines. I'm not sure of the right lines, or maybe I do but don't want to ask them.

Sometimes it's difficult to write. Some days are better than others, just like anything else. But I must press onwards. I bought some potted plants for the condo a couple days ago. I wanted to do something mundane, and it has always helped to buy plants in winter to remind me that growth is possible, even when the earth is hard with ice. When I entered the plant shop to the ringing of the overhead bell, it was empty. Apparently, winter is a killer month in more ways than one. A nice elderly lady with steel-grey hair greeted me at the door as if she had all the time in the world.

"And what are we looking for today?"

Apart from the fact that she worked in a plant shop, I could tell from something in her face that she did gardening outdoors. She had a countenance that allowed me to imagine her in a wide-brimmed hat, bending over to tend flora in the sun.

"To tell you the truth, I really don't know."

"Is it a gift for someone?" Her eyes twinkled, perhaps with a visualized knowledge she'd cooked up inside her head. Being cooped up in a shop all day with few customers could lead to a vivid imagination, one that she might be willing to try out on me.

"No, I just thought I might step in and get something for my home. I didn't really give much thought to what I might get." I felt a bit sheepish because I didn't even have a couple names of plants that I wanted to look at.

"Well, I can certainly help with that. I've been doing this for … oh, I don't know … too many years to count. Plants are my life; you can talk to them, and they listen. That helps them to grow too … the conversation, I mean."

"I like plants that listen."

She laughed, her glasses strings flapping against her chest.

"But I just want something that can stay indoors, stays green, and grows."

"Well, listen up, young man. You are doing a good thing for your home, not just for decoration but for assisting in cleaning the environment."

I'd heard that about plants long ago. It already amazed me that a living organism could make its own food from inorganic substances but had neither the power of movement nor any special organs of sensation or digestion. Their ability to cleanse the air was just one more life phenomenon.

"Yes, it's all about the environment now. It's all the rage."

"Let's start with yours. This is a braided ficus," she said, pointing to a plant with a woven stem that looked like one of Maya's cornrow hairstyles, one she'd put in when she was either bored or tired of having her hair processed. She told me once that I could pull off a cornrow, but I wasn't so sure. I usually gauged my hairstyle by work standards, and I wasn't sure that anybody would trust a therapist with braided hair. I could probably chance it on a Saturday when I was mostly at home and away from professional eyes.

"It's easy to care for, and it's known for its adaptability, which makes it popular for indoor gardens."

"I don't really have a garden. I'm just looking for one or maybe two potted plants to brighten the place up and add a bit of life."

"You could start a garden. They are very satisfying ventures."

That I knew, but I wasn't going to get into it because they could be risky business too.

"There are always cacti. They have temperature and moisture adaptability. The plant forms are interesting, and it reminds you of the Southwest. It's a really intriguing group of plants."

Every cactus I saw reminded me of the Westerns I'd watched on television. I loved Westerns. There were Indians, chiefs, and cowboys. You had your bad guys and your good guys, and everything was clear-cut. In the end, the good guys would win the shootout, and the hero would ride off into the sunset on a beautiful and faithful horse named Boy. But I wasn't sure it was a plant I wanted in my home.

"What else do you have?" I walked around, looking from plant to plant.

She showed me a palm with wispy leaves and easy movements suggestive of the tropics. I passed on that and almost took a Chinese evergreen, which she said would be an excellent selection because it was a low-light lover; it was low maintenance, and of course it had an indoor-purifier factor. I passed on the whole lot, including the orchids, and I wondered what—if anything—I would buy. I felt guilt for wasting her precious time and expertise and knew I would have to get something. Even though there was no one else in the store, I would still buy a penance plant.

"Here's the beautiful amaryllis," she said, "otherwise known as the 'yellow goddess.' It's like bringing spring inside because it bears a soft yellow, trumpet-shaped flower with a sprinkling of green at its neck."

It sounded tempting, but she said nothing about adaptability this time, and that was important. I finally settled on what she told me was a ponytail palm. She said it was for people who were neglectful in their watering, and I knew that was me.

"The foliage of this plant comes from an extraordinary, engorged trunk, and it needs little attention to sustain its beauty."

"All right, that's it. I'll take that." I was perhaps too excited to choose something that needed so little care but could still flourish. I don't know if that meant I was uncaring or lacked time, but I was sold on it.

"I can tell that you think you aren't going to water it."

I shrugged. All I knew then was that I wanted something to remind me that the dormancy and death of winter were just temporary. And now I own a potted plant with roots that hold it firmly in place, and it can't be washed away by anything. Hopefully, I won't prove myself wrong by killing it with neglect.

1 March 2006

I had several dreams last night, ones I can't remember. I can only recall that I was thirteen again, and it was my turn to read the poem I'd written.

Dead butterflies cannot fly,
They can't try, I'm going to cry
Why did they have to die?

I can remember only those three lines from the dream, and I can't seem to add to it from memory. But I do remember my classmates saying what a sad poem it was.

Afterwards, at lunch, Paul wanted to know what had inspired the poem. I told him it was loss, and he said that was depressing.

I am dealing with the demise of different things. One of them hangs in a frame by my door. It's a loss and a preservation all at once. I keep a photograph of Debbie by my bedroom door so it's one of the last things I see when I leave the room. It's also the first thing I see. I touch the frame sometimes, and it triggers the memory of perfumes, soft kisses, warm breath, and a host of other exquisite reminiscences that operate like chemicals in my brain, but all this is accompanied with aches and longings that cannot be quelled. The picture provides a sensory experience on a disinterested, hard white wall. It's an intense atmosphere in which space and time are the only dimensions. I speak to her as one speaks to the departed, asking advice and finding solace. *Good morning, good-bye, how was your day? My day was terrible without you.* I do all the talking to it that I couldn't do when she was here. That's my way of holding on.

But I have tried to let go. I've done some things that I'd never done before. I met my wife at the University of Toronto, but when she left, I started playing pickup from all over the place. I met a girl called Michelle at a club in the entertainment district. There are rules, man rules, about dating girls you meet in certain places, and if you break the policies, unpleasant things can happen. One of the rules is that you never ask a girl out in a club; the semidarkness, smokes, sirens, flashing lights—not to mention the illusions that alcohol provides—mean you might get surprised in the light of day. The exception, of course, is if it's going to be a one-night stand.

So overall, you take your chances whenever you pick up a girl in a club. But Michelle looked hot, and she looked the same in the daylight, so I decided to take her out for dinner at Beijing on Spadina. She told me she loved Chinese food, and I liked Chinatown. On Spadina, just about anything can happen: cheap food, cheap clothes, the latest movies for the lowest prices, and lots of entertainment. She came in, looking dark and yummy, microbraids, red dress, and semi-high heels. She had the confidence that some black women have, the one that says, "I am beautiful, but I can kick your ass if I need to."

"So, John, are you analyzing me right now?" she asked once we were seated and the food came. Almost everybody I met, if they knew I studied psychology, asked me that question at some point, as if that's all I ever could or wanted to do with my time. But nobody is ever just one thing; we are all multi-dimensional creatures, thinking about different things at different times.

"No, I usually leave work at work. That sort of thing takes up too much effort, and I prefer to relax and get to know a beautiful woman instead of examining her with a view to interpreting. Know what I mean?"

"I was hoping for an analysis."

She told me she worked as a massage therapist in the downtown area, so she was in the business of helping people, a remedial business, just like I was. I've heard a lot of things about the massage business, but she looked like a wholesome professional. I didn't think I'd see her as a shady news item on prime time television.

"If I were forced to, I would say the verdict is pretty good. Your head seems to be screwed on right. But I would much rather talk about your profession. Who are the people who get massages?"

She laughed. "Just about anybody who feels they need one. There's no special type or anything. You could get one."

"Could I?"

I watched her hands as she ate the sweet-and-sour spareribs and wondered how many bodies her hands had touched. Was there a cleansing process she followed after each massage, and did she strictly adhered to it?

"Yes, the benefits are endless, especially for someone like you who is in a stressful, emotional job. It reduces fatigue, increase circulation, decreases anxiety, and if you have trouble sleeping at nights, it can help with that too."

She did a good job of promoting; it sounded as if her words could have come straight from a brochure. Maybe they were in a brochure.

"Sounds good, but I could get one of those chairs that do the same thing. I hear they are pretty good, and they get better with each model they make."

"That could do it." She raised her eyebrows as if curious. "However, a mechanical substitute can never produce the exact feeling of a personal, human touch." She touched my hands as she said this, and my fork clattered to the ground as I jumped back. It was too soon in the date for anybody to be touching.

"Sorry. I guess I just didn't expect the contact."

"I don't have thorns on my hand, you know. You don't need a chair; you really do need hands. Maybe it's the stress we've been talking about. You're probably tense from carrying around all those head problems. I have it easy. I do a physical massage, and that's it. You do a mental one, and you still have it with you. You know, if you did get a massage, it would give you a sense of perspective, clarity, and some of peace of mind. Call it an emotional bodywork."

"I could get all that for seventy dollars?"

"Trust me, you can. I get one of the other therapists to do me from time to time, and I am a whole different person afterwards. It works wonders."

I wouldn't get one of the therapists or psychologists to see me; I would write my own analysis. I'd heard about therapists who see other therapists, and I didn't want to be in that category. As one of the only black counsellors, that would be all I needed. In any case, I felt that this was my problem to work out.

It would be just like me to take out a massage therapist, someone who liked to touch. In fact, it was her business to feel. Sometimes, we run towards the very thing we are running from. The subconscious is so strong. Michelle the masseuse, her surname escapes me, told me that massage could pump oxygen and nutrients into tissues and vital organs, improving circulation and increasing my range of motion. All of that sounded absolutely essential to my very existence. But I was interested in how motion could help me get in touch with who I was. I wouldn't find out from her because that was the last time I saw her. I was shamefaced from my awkward reaction to her touch, and although she was interesting, I wasn't interested. I guess I wasn't letting go; I was holding on.

3 March 2006

My nights are filled with dreams now, dreams that are jumbled up and hard to remember except for snatches here and there. It's almost as there are dreams stacked away somewhere just waiting for the floodgates to be opened. I spend more time at work, more time with mind-numbing movies and in bars to shorten the quiet times. Funny, in all those stress-management seminars I attended, that's what they said I needed—quiet time. Now that I have started to write down the acts and the words, there's an outflow of memories, and quiet time compounds this.

Once the dam is broken, it's hard to stop the flow. Some evenings I go home, and the quiet of the house allows my thoughts to go unrestrained. I hear the echoes of my past. High school was challenging: having to contend with girls on a daily basis, liking them but not knowing what to do about them. Still, they were everywhere, at school barbeques, fairs, fetes, the neighbourhood, the library. I found myself around them enough to be called John the Baptist. They thought I was in my own world. And even now I am still crying in the wilderness. I still don't know the things I need to do to move past ten. Heal thyself.

Back when we were near the end of high school, Paul told me he had given up his boyhood.

"What do you mean?"

"You know!"

"Oh yea, me too."

"Well, I'll be—who was it?'

"Nobody special, just some girl I met on holidays last year."

"So you had a bite of the big apple, or did it bite you instead?"

"Either way, the innocence is gone."

It was the start of the lies—or the continuation of them—blended with the secrets. But then, lies and secrets were an extension of each other. There was no girl in New York. I had lifted the skirts of a couple at school, but I wanted to distance myself from that, and New York seemed like a feasible scapegoat. It was near enough but far away, and this phantom girl, whom I had concocted, would be anonymous.

My mother was the custodian of so-called precious heirloom and art. She wanted me to sit in her rocking chair so it would get some use and keep it from dry rotting. Now I was to be the ventilator and keeper of her chair. Of course, I couldn't sit in it anymore. What was exasperating was her lack of awareness about why I couldn't do it.

"If you don't use it, you lose it."

I wondered if she felt that way about everything else.

"Why can't you sit in it? I don't think that's too much to do for your mother. I'd sit myself, but I'm afraid I'm too heavy." My head screamed—she should know the amount of weight it could take.

"I don't like the rocking motions."

"What on earth are you saying? You used to rock that chair so much I thought it would fall apart. I thought my dear mother and grandmother were turning in their graves."

They would roll over for me, but not for her. Now, that was funny, but not in an amusing way. My grandparents were killed in a motor-vehicle accident while driving from Toronto to Buffalo. That's all I knew about them. I was six at the time. I had seen a range of photographs, from the old black-and-whites of their Jamaican days to the coloureds of Toronto. They could be rolling in their graves, but only because they had missed the family reunion they were going to in the Bronx, and because they had met a violent death.

"Anymore. I don't like to rock anymore; it makes me sick like seasickness, I think."

That wasn't the answer I'd wanted to give. I wanted to say, "Mom, I am literally sick from seeing that chair because somewhere in there is broken innocence, torn and destroyed. And it cannot be retrieved. I'll never mend. Death happened while rocking." And as I know from everything that's happened with her, there are a million ways to die, especially on the inside. She was afraid of her chair being broken, and I was afraid my spirit was broken. I saw it lying dead on the lawn outside.

"What do you know about seasickness? Have you ever been on a boat or a ship to know what seasickness is? That poor cat, it's only by the grace of God that you didn't break one of her legs with that chair and your incessant rocking. It's a testament to the strength of the workmanship. They don't build things like they use to. I don't know when you developed this phobia; it certainly seems like it was overnight, and it's a bit curious. So you'll get sick?"

"Yes."

"You are much too delicate for a boy. There has to be some way to toughen you up. If you're going to get motion sickness from sitting in a chair, then I don't know how you're going to survive in this world, but there is time yet."

It was part true, part lie. I did get sick whenever I saw that offending piece of furniture. It creaked continually, at school, in my sleep, on holidays, and in the car when my mother was driving me to school. But it was another lie added to the ever-building spiral I thought I could control somehow. I had two faces and by extension two selves, the inner ones that knew the truth, and the exterior ones, the ones I showed everybody else. Control is false, however, and sometimes the two selves merged. It was the same body, trying to dull the nagging pain, and the same body, showing a painless face.

5 March 2006

I could barely open my eyes this morning, although I had my full quota of eight hours sleep, like the experts say we should get. From somewhere deep below awakening, I heard the little bedside radio saying, "It has one of the longest titles in history," and then the announcer gave out some long song titles from the past, "and now this song that I'm about to play for you is by U2—'Stuck in a Moment You Can't Get Out Of.'" Then on came Bono singing, and I can see the whole gang of them, the Edge and the other two. When I was finally able to get up, the song stayed with me, never leaving me for the whole day. It's a catchy song, but I think my relating to it so much is the reason why it will not go away. I am stuck in a moment I can't get out of. Or can I?

Everything seems to point to my pain now—songs I hear on the radio, programmes I see on TV, movies, even art. I know they were there all along, but it's as if my whole being was asleep, and I am just now slowly waking up to the sights and sounds around me, slowly waking up to *me*. I remember seeing an art catalogue of some works that were being exhibited at a gallery on Queen Street. It must have been my mother's. She would go to all these art exhibitions, as she often said, to *appreciate*. Being in the business, I guess she also had to keep herself informed.

The art gallery she owned was called Radicals, and it featured new age art made of metals, glass, and any other scraps that could be fashioned into something beautiful. It was art by default. Some were installations that I couldn't always figure out. I'd seen one with sheaves and sheaves of paper along with a computer, apparently a suggestion that despite advances in technology, trees were still being killed so we could write and print words. I looked at it, and I wanted to take the papers up for tidiness and put the computer to better use. But what struck me in that catalogue was a piece entitled *The Rapes,* a piece in which I saw myself. Art reflecting life, and life reflecting art—that sort of thing. I saw a girl—well, maybe she could have been a boy—running in happiness and laughter, but then this joyousness abruptly turned into a fit of intense terror and screams. The piece was so vivid, I thought, *My God, but this is me.* I wondered where the artist had gotten the idea. What was his inspiration for *The Rapes*?

There were so many rapes going on, not just of bodies and lands. There was the rape of the spirit; this was the biggest one, a whole many people getting violated by one act. Wedding vows, the sanctity of marriage, even the body was assaulted. One screaming, horror-filled child could ruin a family. The child in that work of art could scream, thank God for that, but my screams were swallowed. I still saw my mother's hand, and every time I heard the creaking of the chair, I knew what was happening. Since that day, everything had been swallowed, and I heard, saw, and felt everything as if from under murky water.

When I saw that piece as a teenager, it struck me as dead on, and I've always remembered it. Today I went downtown to see it, in a mad rush to find something—anything—since I was stuck in a moment. I paid the $10.00 and came face-to-face with *The Rapes*. It was unspeakably real, almost grotesque. This realness transported me back to my own horrors, to the oddity of seeing butterflies that could not fly, to the rocking, to the creaking, and to my muffled existence. I went to a gallery filled with art, and I saw only the one piece. I was blind to everything else. I couldn't show appreciation, when all I felt was violation.

When I was fifteen, I received a letter from my science teacher, which was to be given to my mother. The letter explained why I was being given detention two evenings in a row, something to do with my refusal to participate in the class. I had to explain to my mother that Mr. Burgess wanted me to rip apart and examine dead insects, and I couldn't do it.

"Why do we have to kill insects so we can inspect them?"

"Well, Mr. Clarke, we can't very well examine them if they are flying about the place, can we?" Mr. Burgess circled my desk much the same way I imagined the insects were trapped before the kill. "Do you think they would lie still for us?"

"I don't suppose so, sir, but there must be some other way we could get to know the anatomy of insects."

"No, Mr. Clarke, there's no other way. It's only in death that we have free rein over anything."

He brought his face close to mine to emphasise the word *death*.

"Oh," I said, thinking him cold.

After I left the gallery to hurry back to work, I felt full and light all at once. And I thought that if I allowed myself to sink under the burden of violation, I would remain reserved and in my state of inertia. And although I wasn't ten anymore, in the certain death that I was headed to, that day with the rocking chair would have free rein over me.

6 March 2006

My mother did not like dealing with nuisances, or—as she often put it—things that needlessly interrupted her days. Receiving a letter from Mr. Burgess fell in the category of nuisances.

"Why can't you be a good, regular, fifteen-year-old boy, and just cut open those damn insects? They're dead, for God's sake. Do you think that they're going to come back to life? Must everything be drama with you? Things get cut and sometimes mutilated; that's just the nature of life. Hopefully, some bright, creative soul comes along and takes that mutilation and turns it into something beautiful to look at."

She caressed one of her art pieces and sighed. It was a habit associated with her occupation. Those same hands had driven me to school, rendering me a service. She drove with skill too, confident in her abilities, without the consternation shown by many women I saw holding the steering wheel too stiffly, as if any sort of relaxation would result in a fatal crash. She was offensive and defensive all at once. We hardly conversed in the car. But every now and again, I would glance at her hands on the steering wheel. They were incredibly sensuous, elegant hands that had seen and done a lot.

"But destruction happens. It's the law of the jungle that only the strong survive. I thought they taught you about the survival of the fittest in school. Maybe that's what the man's trying to tell you, but you just stick your head in the sand with all these idealistic notions you have in that head of yours. I must be the only mother who got this letter. Every boy I know likes to cut stuff up, but not you."

"I just don't understand why I must—"

"That has always been a problem with you—your constant need to understand all things. Take this life lesson from your mother: If you continue trying to understand everything, you will end up at a place where you don't want to be. Just accept some things as they are."

"Is that who you really want me to be—someone who just accept things without question?"

"Sometimes acceptance gives you peace of mind."

I wanted to ask her if she had peace of mind, but I knew that her answers would just frustrate me as my questions would equally frustrate her.

"But, Mom, what about curiosity? What about the need to know?"

"What about it? Use it in your science class to look inside those insects. The pictures you see in textbooks didn't come from some man's imagination; it came from a dead insect that gave its life to further the pursuit of knowledge. I don't want to receive any more letters or notes, and I don't want to be called to your school. There aren't enough minutes in the day to be losing time over your failure to accept the world as it is. At fifteen, you are almost a man. Get used to seeing things die."

She wheeled away, leaving only a trail of smoke and a living room of silence. I was used to quiet. Everything was quiet with the upper-middle-class. Quiet neighbourhood, quiet drives to school with my mother. Everything hushed. I wondered if it would be different if I lived elsewhere, somewhere else in Toronto where I could scream my head off, and it wouldn't hurt the landscape.

Why did she have to kill things? I wondered. Back when I was seven, I was disappointed and more than a little angry that my father had to leave, but as I grew older, I understood that he had his art and his dreams; he was a free spirit and could not be pinned down in Forest Hill. My mother had told him Toronto did not need another reggae-ska-pop singer—or whatever genre he was into. My father told her the world didn't need reggae, rock, or pop singers; the world needed poetry and soulfulness, and that's what he was going to give it. I wish I had inherited some of his soulfulness; it would probably have helped me to open up to my feelings. Instead, I feel soulless.

11 March 2006

One good thing might come out of my confrontation with *The Rapes*: I will see more because I am looking for meaning in the works. I will not just see colour and form; I am searching for a brush stroke that will connect with something inside me and give me clarity. I have always gone to art galleries and exhibition openings; I am my mother's child, after all. Maya and I usually make an event of it, and even though we invite Paul, he resists. He says that although he can appreciate his share of art, he finds galleries notoriously pretentious and out of touch with the common man. I agree to some extent, but I ignore the toffee-nosed ambience and go about my business appreciatively. We mostly go on Sundays, and Paul will say he has to go to church, which we all know is a blatant lie.

Paul is only interested in going to church if there is a girl there that he has some interest in. Consequently, he goes to many different churches of various denominations. He's even found himself at a Calvinist church once or twice. He suddenly started following the teachings of John Calvin, a French Protestant religious reformer who lived in Switzerland. The only thing Paul hadn't told us about Calvin was the years he had lived. Not surprisingly, Maya is interested in art and usually calls to find out if I am going and which gallery we will be going to. She is a fly girl, with the new bob and the Revlon hair colour. She is always happening, and art is as eclectic to her as food is.

I go looking for the creative activity and the production of imaginative ideas and designs, as if I could obtain inspiration for an outlet of release. I told Maya as much one Sunday.

"If you find release in them, that's great. Whatever works. But I thought it was the artists who get that release."

"If the viewer cannot identify with a piece, then what would be the fun of seeing the works? They are all stories."

"I see, but what exactly are you releasing? You have released yourself from a marriage you say is irreconcilable, and you are writing about it. You are writing about your conversations and interaction with Aunt Martha. That's your release too. You are writing, aren't you?"

"Yes, but I need more."

"More of what? You are losing me, kiddo."

"More open spaces, more room to breathe."

That was how I felt, physically and mentally: that my breathing space was contracted, closing in on me. And strangely enough, these exhibitions with their spaciousness, the art with their creative resourcefulness, gave me the sense that I could stretch beyond the boundaries and forge my own channel of deliverance.

"Breathing is up to you. It's as simple as inhaling and exhaling. Try it." She feigned breathing motions by heaving her chest in an exaggerated manner.

There was a time when I thought I had asthma, but doctors could never find it, and over a period of years, I went through the same questions.

"Have you been doing any strenuous exercise lately?"

"No."

"Are you stressed at school or work, as in any additional duties?"

"No."

"Is there anything you are allergic to?"

"No."

"Have you lifted anything heavy recently?"

"No."

The questions continued over years, and finally my doctor said there was nothing wrong with me; it was psychological. Well, I laughed and said I didn't have psychological problems. Ventolin, the handheld inhaler used by asthmatics, became my constant companion, and my difficulty in breathing continued. It became especially exacerbated when I had to be in close contact with people, even in elevators. I find I have needed Ventolin less since Debbie left and I could be myself. This is a sad commentary and realization.

I never use Ventolin in public because it reminds me of being a child. Somehow a successful therapist and Ventolin don't go well together, especially since I don't have asthma. How would I explain? *So, you have asthma? Well, no, but I can't breathe.* Strangely enough, Debbie complained that Ventolin kept coming between us because most of the times she tried to get intimate, I suddenly couldn't breathe. I would reach for the ventilator and give myself a spurt. *Not now, Debbie, I can't breathe. You're too heavy; I can't breathe. I can't breathe. I can't breathe.* Well, maybe Ventolin can become your lover; just blow and go. So now I need the space not just to inhale but to find inspiration for release, to heal. How do you find that in an art gallery?

14 March 2006

Debbie was the kind of woman most men want. She was intelligent, smart, beautiful, and independent. She also had a name in a major Toronto newspaper. When I asked her to marry me and she said yes, I felt a sense of accomplishment. I should have felt joy, but accomplishment would cut it for me. In the end, when we parted, the accomplishment went away with her. And of course, her independence didn't help. I tried to appease myself by offering her things. I told her the condo we bought together had appreciated in cost, so I would give her more money. No, she wouldn't take a cent more than half of what was hers. I upped the ante. Take the condo. No, her half of the money was just fine.

So there was no appeasing myself. I was left with everything that I owned and everything that I came into the marriage with. Perhaps if Debbie had taken everything I'd offered, I would feel no better, but I wanted the satisfaction of giving her something—anything—to make up for everything I did not and could not give her. It was as if I wanted to pay compensatory damages for the harm I caused her. Or maybe it was for a breach of the marriage contract, since I didn't love her as much as I was capable of doing.

She tried. She really did. Debbie bought books and videos on intimacy. They were materials geared towards learning in a different way. One day, she had one of those books in the living room. I think it was a Saturday or Sunday morning. She was making coffee in the kitchen.

"I thought we could go through that book together."

I cringed inside, and maybe on the outside too. *Discovering Change through Intimacy* was not a book I wanted to go through. The word *change* was also a little frightening.

"How many of these books are we going to read?" The kettle's shrill whistle broke into my thoughts and made me irritable.

"I don't know, John—maybe no more, or maybe many more until we've done enough to see some change."

She poured steaming water in her cup and looked at me quizzically. I didn't know what to say. I didn't want to fight, but I could feel my defence mechanisms kicking in. Maybe it was fear, but fear of what I didn't know.

"Well."

"Well, what?" I asked, thinking of a way to bolt.

"When can we go through the book together?" She sipped the coffee, made a face, and decided to add more sugar.

"I don't have the time now." I watched her hand with the spoon repeatedly stirring the liquid inside the cup. I knew that trouble was brewing, and I also saw that each stir was similar to the number of times we would be having conversations like these.

"It's the weekend. What do you have to do?"

I could see through the kitchen window little clumps of grass pushing themselves out of the earth, sure signs of growth.

"I have some things to do." I rushed off to my car and drove away with my shaky protection and my ever-present fear. I chose to run away rather than stay and do battle.

This was what I wanted to compensate her for—all the bloody times that she had tried and failed, and all the times that I had taken flight.

15 March 2006

I keep reading what I've written to see the self-discovery in it. I don't fully see it, but I see connections. The second time I stumbled upon my mother doing what I came to realize was a regular activity, I wondered why she did it. Actually, it was a while before I wondered this. My first thought was to wonder how I could avoid seeing it again. If she needed love, there was Henry. Maybe she needed more. But more of what?

I thought of all the things a boy could give his mother to make her be the person he thought she was or wanted her to be. I gave her better grades, more assistance around the house, peace and quiet—but none of that helped. I thought that if I brought my friends over most days, she would be forced to stop from pride or embarrassment. I was wrong again. Boys running around in her space only made her agitated.

"John, dear, this is not a playground. I am sure they are not strays. Your friends have homes, don't they?"

"Yes, but they like it here."

"So do I. And I plan to keep liking it. I wonder—what's so special about this place?"

"We have more space."

"Well, I need my space. I don't want your friends over more than once a week, and I need to know beforehand when they are coming. Even playgrounds have rules."

I knew then that my plans had failed.

"Do you remember the time we went to Vancouver and we saw those butterflies?"

"Yes, such beautiful yet fragile creatures. They die so quickly. But perhaps they wouldn't know what to do with an extended lifespan since all they do is fly—or flit, flit, flit—from place to place." As she spoke, she flapped her hands in imitation of a butterfly's bouncing, irregular flight.

"I don't know, Mom, they migrate back and forth when the seasons change. Sometimes they travel for thousands of miles. And some of them live for up to a year, depending on the species."

"My dear boy, you tend to see things with such a slanted view. You are so inventive. It's not the same ones that return, you know. But that was a long time ago." She waved her free hand to show time passing. "Why on earth are we talking about this now?"

"Because it was a nice trip."

"Well, good. If I could enjoy the space in my home without the constant intrusion of your little friends, I'll be good too."

After that, what could I do but leave her with her space and the freedom to do whatever she wanted with that space.

What did I do with the seed mix I brought home from the Vancouver Aquarium? I built my own garden in the backyard. Forest Hills was the right kind of place for one. There were lots of trees, rotten fruits on the ground, and compost. I wasn't sure what exactly the mix contained, but somebody told me there had to be milkweeds in there. Evidently, it was a plant popular with butterflies. I wanted to see every stage of the butterfly's life at my convenience: eggs, caterpillars, pupas, and then butterflies. Plus, I had heard that butterflies visited these plants when they bloomed because they were attracted to the nectar. Either way, I would have some butterflies.

That autumn, I turned eight and planted all the seeds I had. And when my world seemed to be falling apart, I really worked at the garden. I thought that if I had a beautiful garden with butterflies, I could somehow transfer that beauty into my life. I was told that the plants might not look as good as I would like until the second year, so I wanted to get cracking. I think that was the longest winter for me, waiting for spring to arrive to see if I would have any plants and how big they would be. They weren't big, and they didn't have big blooms, but the butterflies came. I saw the eggs, and I saw the caterpillar eating the leaves. The pupal stage was ugly to look at, and I could not wait for that part to be over, but knowing that beauty was at the end of it made waiting easier. My mother did not say a lot while all this was going on, except to say, "Try not to bring any dirt from outside; this house is a bitch to keep clean." Once my Aunt Daphne came over and asked with much delight, "John did all this?"

"Yes," my mother said, "he's very good at these sorts of things. If he takes to something, he doesn't let it go, and he nurtures the idealistic. I thought that like everybody else who got those seeds he would just throw them away or forget about them, but of course I was wrong. I should have known better."

"Well, there's nothing wrong with dedication or idealism. Without idealism, the world would be quite an ugly place to live in. I think it's quite beautiful."

"That it is, but it won't last."

I asked my aunt why that one stage of the butterfly's development was so ugly.

"Well, every stage can't be the same."

"But all the other ones aren't bad to look at. I know stages are supposed to be different, but this one isn't pleasant."

I was also thinking that apart from the ugliness, there was not much to see because there was not a lot of activity going on. The pupae just sat there in neutral.

"John, as ugly as they are, that stage is the time when the adult structure is formed. You know those beautiful things you love to see flying about? Without this stage, I don't know what would happen. That unattractive hard coating is protection from any danger that might affect the butterflies."

After that, I didn't enjoy the pupal stage any better, but I gained a deeper appreciation for what it meant. The trip to Vancouver was meaningful for me, and it turned out to be fruitful, but there was also something about the different stages of the butterfly that I wanted to hold onto. I wanted that metamorphosis to extent itself into my home life. I was eager for the butterflies, but I seemed to be stuck at the pupae. I wasn't even sure if that was where I was, since everything was just the same as before. Why did some stages take so long to be worked out? And why was there so much ugliness before beauty could emerge?

16 March 2006

Only a day has passed since my last entry. I sit and stare at the journal with my thoughts flowing but my pen unmoving. I have a folded copy of the *Chronicle* beside the journal. I have never had such a great urge to read Debbie's columns as I do now; it's as if by reading them I could have the relationship we never had when we were married. And sometimes I say out loud, "She was here," like the way I see variations of the phrase carved in a tree truck or scribbled on the seat of a train. I have a framed photograph to prove it. I used to discuss her articles with her. That was one thing I could do—participate in a conversation. If conversations about current affairs could have saved us, we would still be married.

I have become obsessed with getting the *Chronicle*. If I don't get it, I call Maya and tell her I need her copy when she is finished with it. She always brings it to me without question, but I think she knows that something is going on. Last week was the last time I asked her. I called her from my office.

"I know they are cutting back on extras to scrape a penny here and there, but don't they deliver papers to the government offices anymore?"

"Yea, but somebody must have snatched it. I don't know. I just need to get the chronic." I looked at my desk, piled high with cases I needed to work on; I knew I shouldn't be taking any time away from them to read the paper.

"Funny you should say chronic, like it was a long-lasting disease or a bad habit. John, you know you could call her up."

"Who?"

"Don't act like a man and pretend you don't know what I am talking about. *Debbie!* What is it with you and acting ignorant?" Maya seemed a bit impatient. I was glad she was on the phone, and we were not having a face-to-face.

"First of all, I am a man. Somehow, I seem to have to keep telling people that, and secondly—what would I be calling her for?" It seemed my patience was on the edge too, but I had to calm down because I needed her to bring the paper.

"The same reason you have to read what she says every single day, like it's the gospel or something. You have to get your Debbie fix."

"It's no fix. I've always enjoyed her articles." That was the truth too; I had always enjoyed seeing my wife's name in the paper and reading what she had to say. Sometimes I would discuss her articles with her, but that was long ago, when my inadequacies were not yet highlighted.

"Yes, you have, but you seem to be enjoying them more by the day."

"Her writing gets better with time. I don't want to be cliché, but it's like fine wine."

"I see what you're doing, and I don't have enough time in the day to pursue this kind of evasion. Hopefully you'll feel better when you call her."

"I can't."

"Can't, or won't? You seem to be unwilling to do a lot of things that are in your hands. You just have to do it. I don't want to be cliché," she mocked me, "but don't think—just do it." Here was yet another sports motto thrown at me. We all have to thank Nike for the inspiration.

"I just don't know what I would say to her right now."

"I'll bring the paper to you on my way home." Maya was finished with me. The tone of her voice told me I was dismissed. I guessed she was tired of the futility of a conversation that was going nowhere.

I told Maya the truth. I have nothing to say to Debbie. We have not talked about anything but assets since the split, nothing about why everything fell apart. When I think about it, I should have been the one doing all the talking.

20 March 2006

I spent the two nights of the weekend at the True Words café. It was our spot. I've never known the rationale behind the name; maybe it means that if you drink enough, you start to speak the truth. Didn't work for me. Maya was late on Friday. She had a "thing" with her girlfriends first. (I put the pen down for a moment to wonder why I am writing about hanging out at bars and what good all of this writing will do for me. I am staring at her photo in the *Chronicle*, and I am seeing my mother's hands.) And I know with the clarity of hindsight that it was those hands that stretched through so many years to come between me and the woman I loved. I guess I have always known this. That's why I hated it when she asked me about repairing my marriage: She played a hand in bringing it to disrepair. Yet I have always wanted to heal things and to repair them.

"Mom, do you love Henry?"

She took a deep breath and released it. *"What is this now, an inquisition?"*

"I just want to know."

"You're ten years old. Why should love concern you?" Her voice was filled with years of tobacco, and her fingers clutched a Virgie. Sometimes she would play jazz on the stereo, and then a woman would sing with a voice that sounded like heavy, billowing smoke. Their raspy feel reminded me of each other.

"Concern yourself with survival, and leave love alone. That's the problem with you and your father—always trying to save and heal the world. You with your gardens and butterflies in your head, and

him with his teaching of music and the rest of it. You don't know how to just live and get by."

This is what I didn't understand: a curator of a gallery who could not appreciate restoration. She loved music too, and apart from smoky voice, she would play Billie Holiday over and over. I knew the words to "The Man I Love" and "Who Wants Love" by heart. At ten, I could sing the blues because I had heard them so often.

"Get by what?"

"Disappointments and heartaches."

"I think that you should love Henry more, and maybe you could stop—"

"Stop what!" She puffed furiously at the fast-fading cigarette. I glanced around to avoid her direct glare and looked at all the expensive pieces made from twisted metal that occupied the room. Still, I forged ahead.

"Maybe you could make a sacrifice." I pushed ahead even though I saw anger in her eyes.

"Boy, do you know what a sacrifice is? It's standing right in front of me—you! You are a sacrifice. I have a scar down the middle of my abdomen from a C-section, weight I have not lost for years, and I have been carrying you around like a goddamn handbag for the past ten years, so don't talk to me about love and sacrifice. I make bloody sacrifices every day."

"I wasn't talking about me; I was talking about Henry."

"Did Henry ask you to speak for him?"

"No, but since he doesn't know, he can't speak for himself."

She took a step closer to me, putting her hands on the sides of my face, still clutching the smoke stick between her fingers. The *rising smoke caressed my face. "I am so tired of telling you the same thing—stop interfering with things that do not concern you. Start toughening up. Do you have a dick between your legs?" The hand of smoke descended and squeezed. For a moment, I forgot about Henry and thought about my penis and balls being set on fire. "Oh, they're still there. Now start acting like you have a pair." As usual, I was left with a screen of smoke and now-smarting balls.*

My mother has been squeezing my balls from that day. And what have I been doing?

When Maya finally came Friday night, her radars were up.

"You don't look so good."

"I don't feel so well."

"You have not been well for a while."

"What's that suppose to mean?"

"I am sure you know what I mean. Typical John—no clue what's happening. You know, you're only fooling yourself, and you've been doing that for a long time."

"Wait. Time out. Am I imagining things, or are you on my case? Were you and your girlfriends bashing men, and now I am an extension of this?"

"When have you ever known me to bash men, as you call it? You are beginning to sound like Paul, who thinks we are always man bashing or on the rag. Because—obviously—I can't say what I feel without bleeding. Okay, let's drop this. I have no business meddling in your personal life."

But of course, she did have that right. I did know what she was getting at. She was the only one I had told my story to. Every so often, she would say something profound, and I would find some way to wriggle out of the tight space she tried to put me in. What kind of man was I, who couldn't fix his own life and who always pointed his finger at his mother?

People said I looked like her. In another life, that would have been a huge compliment. But now I wasn't sure of how I felt about that. If I had looked like my father, that would have been fine because he was a man, but looking like her—that was something else. I didn't know what to do with the fact that I resembled her. If I resisted everything about her and still had to see her when I looked at myself in the mirror, then there would be no escape. Funny, if anybody had spoken about the resemblance before I was ten, I would have soaked it up, even basked in it.

Now I look at her and think I am looking at myself. If she looked like me, why couldn't she act right?

"You are the splitting image of your mother," Paul said many times, even when we were younger.

"Great."

"You know what they say about boys who look like their mothers." It was a statement because he thought I knew what the saying was.

"What do they say?"

"That they are lucky."

"Yea, well I'm still waiting. Where did that saying come from, anyway?"

"Jamaica. All of our sayings are from there, don't you know? They have the best sayings for all sorts of situations, and they are usually true too."

"Even Jamaicans can be off sometimes."

Paul was one of the friends I tried to use as a buffer against my mother's activities. He didn't know she had ordered me to not invite them over so many times. He didn't know I had to tell her long in advance of any impending visits so she could fix her schedule. I sometimes wondered that if he had known what was going on, would he still have thought I was lucky? He also thought I was fortunate because she was beautiful. I thought she was beautiful too, but I knew she was infected inside—like an apple that looks great until you bite into it and see the worms.

Still, I couldn't live down the comments that we had swapped heads. Since I didn't like it, I thought of ways I could make her go away, as if I could erase the genes. I kept myself clean shaven most times for much of my life, but then I thought that if facial hair could help me erase my mother from my face, I would use it. So I grew a goatee and sideburns, but I decided that a moustache would be too much to tolerate. Sometimes I confused myself with the duality of trying to be clean shaven but wanting to have the accessories of manhood. At one point in our marriage, Debbie thought it might have been a fashion statement.

"Are you supposed to be Freud?"

"He had a beard perhaps; this is a goatee. It's much more complex than the standard beard."

"Oh, right, Mr. Complexity, the huge difference escaped me. My apologies for getting the two mixed up. You are from clean to this; what's your inspiration?"

"Something to tickle you with."

"Mmmm, wouldn't that be lovely? I didn't think trendy haircuts were your thing, but it doesn't look bad. The thing is, goatees and sideburns are high maintenance. You've got to be at the barber practically every week."

"I guess I am a high-maintenance man."

I couldn't tell her that a man of twenty-six was hiding behind a goatee. It was a goatee mask.

"All right, a complex, high-maintenance man who has a goatee and not a beard and who isn't Freud."

I didn't think she knew it, but even her reference to Freud touched a nerve. Of all the names of bearded men she could have chosen, she chose Freud. The man was a master on the subject of things repressed. And the defence mechanism of facial hair was like a boomerang; people always saw past the camouflage because they still commented on the resemblance, and as soon as this happened, I was clean shaven again.

I was not the only one who looked in mirrors for self-analysis or change; Debbie did too, and she told me about it.

"I looked in the mirror, John, and I didn't like what I saw."

"What do you mean?"

"I don't like myself in this relationship anymore. It seems as if my daily routine revolves around fixing you, and I can't do it. I'm not even sure if you want to be fixed."

I didn't tell her then that men did not get into relationships to be fixed. We just want to be.

"What about me needs fixing?"

"I don't think I can do this anymore. I have become someone I'm not, thinking that if I love you enough, work hard on our relationship, that you'll become the way I want and everything will work—but it's not working."

It would be so much easier to get the man you wanted to begin with, rather than try to make adjustments to the one you had. I never cheated on my wife, but she said she felt emotionally cheated. When she started with her mirror analogy, I knew that the end was near, that she had run into enough brick walls.

25 March 2006

I learnt the art of secrecy while very young. It's really an art, a skill I honed. Ironically, I spend my days trying to get people to come clean. That was a problem in the marriage too: I couldn't come clean. Not only was I secretive but I projected this onto Debbie. What was she doing when I wasn't around?

I would go through her drawers and her things, smell her clothing in her closet, search up and down the condo. I was never sure what I was looking for. In the middle of the workday, even when I was dealing with clients, I had the strong, irresistible urge to go home and see what was happening. Most women are meticulous, and they know if you go through their stuff. They are organized creatures who know where they place every single item, and Debbie was no different—she knew.

"Have you been through my drawers?"

"No, why would I? I have my own drawers."

"I don't know why you would, but this is not how I left my things. Nothing is ever as it seems in this house. I can't leave anything, anywhere. There are only two people living here."

"Maybe there are spirits in here."

"Right. I can't wait to see any one of them, speak to them, and ask them what they are looking for."

That's how it went, until I learnt to organize things the way I found them. This one was folded like that; another one was laid out on top. I didn't find anything. Maybe I was looking for myself. I felt sadness and shame at my self-destructing descent.

Self-destruction didn't end because I pitied myself. It was a road well travelled, and I kept going down the familiar paths, like all people with bad habits. So much for the road less travelled. One place I travelled to often in my marriage was the *Chronicle*; it was like the impulse to go home at all hours of the day. I would go to Debbie's office and wonder whether she knew what I was doing. Parking anywhere close to that office was expensive, so it probably wasn't worth it. I would breeze in, always interrupting some editorial meeting.

"I wish I had known you were coming. I have a meeting in a few."

"I didn't know I was coming. I was just in the neighbourhood."

Just being in her neighbourhood was a bit of a drive and a quite a chunk of change for parking.

"What are you doing down here?"

"You know, the usual meetings here and there."

I usually didn't tell her anything concrete; after all, there was nothing to form any kind of solid excuse for dropping in. An obscure engagement would always do the trick.

"I didn't want to surprise you, but I was already here."

"You are down here a lot. They never seem to have meetings at your office. It must be nice to get away."

"Yes, it's a nice break."

I looked around. I had read or heard somewhere that when women had affairs, they usually had them with someone they worked with. That made sense; that was where they spent most of their time when they weren't at home.

"Nice break for you; surprise visits for me. I love to see you, but your timing is always bad. I see you coming sometimes, and my mind goes into overdrive thinking that something has happened."

"Sorry to alarm you."

"I guess I might be an alarmist because I see you here often enough these days not to feel that something has happened. You should call me ahead of time so I know how to work my schedule around your visits."

I didn't want to call ahead. Planned visits would have been pointless to what I wanted to find out. It was all laughable because there was nothing to find out. There was no logical reason to believe Debbie was cheating. Rationality had a funny way of disappearing when you hang on to past images of a mother who cheated repeatedly.

"I don't know if I'll be coming back down here anytime soon. But if I do, you'll be the first to know."

My visits to her office ended the same way that searching the drawers of her dresser had—with sadness and shame, especially because I was helpless to stop myself from distrusting her. There was no validation of my distrust, only that helplessness, that sadness and shame. I turned my own inadequacies of detachment and fear into a useless quest to find Debbie's. I found nothing.

27 March 2006

Every time I'm about to make an entry in this journal, I hear Paul telling me I've been vaginized. It sounds like a word that really exists, something like *euthanized*—an easy death for a person suffering from a painful, incurable disease. There is no such word, of course; it's just one he coined. Paul, the maker of new words I write in my journal. It has a certain resonance, especially when said out loud, like a word found in the dictionary. Root word *vagina*. Definition: the passage leading from the vulva to the womb in women. Well, I stick my hand between my legs sometimes to be sure it's still there, and then I put pen to paper in my man's journal. Looking back, my personal life was never a part of my marriage. I reread this, and it sounds paradoxical. I left *me* separate. And it is that separateness that was my downfall. But I was taught separateness.

My mother is tall, elegant, and has an elongated neck like that of a swan. Her skin is like the very best chocolate, and she is beautiful. That's what I thought, anyway. But there is an ugliness to her as well, and that is where the separateness comes in. At fifteen, I had my first serious girlfriend. I was on top of the world, constant hard on, constantly checking to see if I was the one by calling her to talk and check on what she was doing. When Charlene told me not to call so much, I fell from dizzying heights to rock-bottom low.

"What's all this moping about?"

"Charlene."

"What about her—is she dead?"

"You are being so morbid right now that I don't know if I should even talk to you. Anyway, she said I called her too much."

"Maybe you do."

"I thought that's what girls wanted—attention."

"Too much of it from one person can be like prison."

"What are you saying?"

"Girls … women … they need space."

"Are you talking about yourself?"

"No, I am talking about females in general. If I was talking about me, I would tell you that I create my own space. Nobody puts me in a box."

"And how do you do that?"

"I keep different parts of my life compartmentalized. I keep certain parts of me for me, and nobody touches those parts."

"What about Henry?"

"What about him? Henry is marriage. I give him what he needs and keep me for me."

"Does Henry know you're giving him just one-eighth of yourself?"

"How did you calculate one-eighth? It could be more, and it could be so much less. And how does any man know how much he's actually getting? How does anybody know how much they are getting? Give the girl her space. There'll be lots of other girls you can turn your attention on. Claustrophobia is a serious thing."

"Who's talking about claustrophobia? I'm talking about giving attention to someone who doesn't want it."

"I rest my case. What do you know about giving anything? Give the females in your life a little space, and maybe you'll get a little piece of them. A little bit is all anybody needs."

"Maybe that's why you are how you are."

"And how am I? Pray tell me. I await this enlightenment by my fifteen-year-old son."

"Dreary in your outlook. You give too little, and you expect very little in return, and that's sad."

She threw her head back and laughed. "What's sad is how much you expect. In time, you'll see how very little return on investment you'll receive for all your romanticism."

As much as I resisted my mother's philosophy, I sucked it in and made it my own. She had taught me not to get close to anyone and I knew from the time I was ten years old that this would be detrimental to any relationship. Yet, here I was, having trouble with closeness. Despite my strongest opposition to my mother's ideas, I somehow succumbed to a blind acceptance of them, and in living with them, I made them into my prison. I never gave all of myself, and on that basis, I guess I couldn't expect to get all of anyone else. Can I write myself out of this cell?

1 April 2006

All Fools' Day. I fit right in. I keep remembering conversations and deeds from long ago. That's what makes us—the things we have heard and the deeds we have seen and what we did afterwards with the two combined. I have seen much more than I wanted to. Sometimes I wonder which I'll come to terms with first—the acts or the words. I moved to my new office without any fanfare. My case load is heavier, and the cases are more complex. I have one central case eating away at me, a toxic mother-and-son relationship.

The son is aggressive; he refuses to do his chores, and he talks back to his mother. Role playing and learning new behaviours through observation don't help. I've decided to give him a gold medal every time he does his chores and acts with less aggression, thus reinforcing the desired behaviour. Herein lay the irony: How can I effectively mend his behaviour when I cannot mend my own? I need a gold medal too. It was only after my marriage disintegrated that I had the courage to say anything at all to anybody. I chose Maya because, in spite of her irreverence, I can talk to her. The girl is as sharp as a whip. The day after Debbie left, I was going out of my mind. Who knows what to do in a house that is devoid of company, empty of furniture, and lacks anything to say? I took Maya out for drinks and broke the news that I was alone again.

"I am sorry to hear that," she said, sniffing at her red wine.

"You don't look or sound surprise." My choice of drink was a beer because I associated it with being male, and I needed to feel masculine.

"Nothing much surprises me these days. Plus, if I can be totally honest, you never seem to be involved."

"Involved in what?" My beer had a big head, and I wondered how much beer I had lost to foam. They say the head is influenced by the kind of starch used to ferment the beer. I didn't care much about fermentation; I just wanted my full quota of beer.

"Your marriage—you seemed sort of aloof, like you were way above it." She took a sip from her glass and wiped the spot where her lipstick smeared, which was weird since it would only be smeared again with the next sip.

"Wow. I didn't know you felt that way. Why didn't you say something?"

I thought about the word *aloof* and couldn't find a way to put a positive spin on it. It just brought to mind separateness again.

"As close as we are, marriage is a private thing. Sometimes meddling can make things worse. I didn't want to cross the line between appreciation and resentment. That line can be very thin. Plus, I'd hope that as time wore on, things would be better. Apart from my parents, you and Debbie are two of my favourite persons."

"So what exactly did you notice?" I took a large swig of the beer, looking around the bar at the inviting and vibrant space and the collection of spirits on display. Some serious salsa beats resonated off the walls.

"As I said, there was an aloofness, like you were in it but not really in it. Why was that, anyway? Did you love her?" Maya spread her palms open as she asked the question.

"I loved her; I just didn't know *how* to love her."

"That sounds so profound I want to write it down and make a song out of it—or save it as an important quote—but what exactly does it mean?"

"I think I have issues."

Maya made a clinking sound on the wine glass with her nails, as if she was going to make an announcement. Apart from the tapping, I saw sarcasm on her raised eyebrows.

"Don't we all? What makes your life so challenging?"

"This is the first time I am going to say this, maybe because I am forced to, or maybe if I say it I put it out there and out of myself. When I was ten, I discovered my mother screwing a man other than my stepfather, and afterwards, many other men. I don't know if she was doing this when she was with my father too, but I am almost sure she was. I tried in my little-boy way to deter her, but to no avail. It seemed her very survival depended on the attention of a variety of men."

I swallowed more of the beer, hoping to wash down and away what I had divulged.

"This is the second time I have to say I'm sorry." She ran her fingers up and down the tall, elegant stem of the wine glass. "That's definitely not a nice thing to find out. Your mother—my aunt—that's out of this world. I have always admired Aunt Martha. She's so beautiful and polished, but who knew she could have two different lives and effectively pull it off without many people knowing?"

"Yea, she is the privileged prostitute of Forest Hill." There were happy people everywhere in the bar—or so it seemed anyway. There were people having martinis and people dancing to the pulsating, rhythmic beats. The bar was sweltering with the sound and feel of salsa. It was everything I wasn't feeling, but it was a good distraction.

"I don't know what to say. I can tell this bothers you a lot. Is this why you are in love but don't know what to do with it?" She raised her eyebrows again. Who knew what to do with every emotion that was felt?

"God, it seems foolish to be affected by this shit even now, to be living my life in this retarded way based on one woman's actions. It's like I'm under a terrible spell." I was on my second beer now, and this one had less head.

"You—more than anyone—should know how some things can affect us for life. Plus, it's your *mother*, for God's sake. She is like your Madonna. But at some point, in some way you are going to have to get over it. You can't keep putting all your shit on her."

"That's it—I don't know how. It's all I know." That was the problem with refuse: Nobody wanted it, always preferring to give it to somebody else.

"Which means you're in your comfort zone." She held both sides of the table and shook it for emphasis. "You need to get un-com-for-table."

"I don't know how."

"I just showed you. Shake things up. You are the therapist with the numerous methods of treatment. You are the one who told me that you create discomfort for others so they can get better. Maybe you need to rehearse something different. I am only a marketing-and-sales manager. I sell; you fix. I would say you are more qualified to make discomfort."

"Everything you say makes sense."

"Debbie doesn't know about this, does she?"

"No." The bar was bathed in a kaleidoscope of bright colours, which added to the whole vibrant, animated ambiance. It was called Act Two, and that was appropriate. I felt that my entire life was staged. I was an actor with a bad script.

"Well, there's a way to get uncomfortable. Give your wife a little piece of yourself. Tell her why you've been so … so aloof. I am using that word a lot, but it does suit you. It's not going to absolve you because—let's face it—you made your own decisions. But she may understand a little, so go talk to your wife."

"One, she is my ex-wife. Two, what good will that do now? She's already gone. Some sorry story will not bring her back. If I say, hey, my mother fucked around, so my head is kind of screwed up—what's going to happen?"

"Well, who knows what will happen? But here's what can happen. She'll understand why the marriage didn't work. There's nothing like a broken relationship where the problem is never identified. Also, it would be good for you to spill something you have been carrying around for a while to someone whom you should have told."

"I don't know about talking to her right now."

Act Two. I considered the name again and its aptness. Maya was trying to tell me that I should move forward. If I were on stage, I could progress to the next act, but I had to take my cue.

"It's up to you, John."

Everything is up to me, and look at the job I've done so far.

4 April 2006

I visited my father often after the split. Of course, I resisted at first, but as I got older, I changed my mind. He tried to make an impact in my life with those visits. I would listen to his new music and give him my critique, and he would listen to what was happening with me and give me his thoughts. I never asked him why he and my mother divorced. By the time I started visiting him, it didn't matter. But I think I got hints here and there. He was seeing someone else, a woman named Joy, and he would sing her praises.

"That Joy, she's a good woman. Always trying to build me up. No dramas. Make sure you find a woman like that. No dream crushers."

"I'll try."

I did find that woman. But back to my father.

"Some women are ball crushers. They will squeeze your balls and make you forget you're a man. You want to steer clear from that."

"Is that what Mom did—bust your balls?"

"A father should never muddy the name of his child's mother, especially not to the child."

"You're trying to protect me."

"It's not about protection. The past is the past, and there's nothing anybody can do about it, so saying something bad about your mother now is pointless. I don't know how much protecting I can do with me being here in Kingston and you being there in Toronto."

He was right. My visits to him were just time-outs.

And I would tell him, "I can take care of myself."

I thought I could.

"You have to be able to. But don't try to be too tough; just because you're male, don't mean you can't feel."

"You mean being sensitive?"

"That, and more."

"Who does sensitive work for? Not me."

"I don't know why you're saying that, but you need sensitivity to be human. Don't forget that. You'll see."

Of course, he was right.

My mother didn't really care about my visits. On my return, she would either say nothing, as if I hadn't gone anywhere, or she would make jibes like, "So, is your father still trying to save the world with his music?"

My writing is beginning to be my reflection. And as I write and think, I wonder whether I would be a different man if I had spent my life with my father. Maybe, and maybe not; it's a toss-up. This is water under the bridge, and I am where I am. And I am who I am. Whatever adjustments I am going to make will have to be made from here.

People come of age, either at eighteen or at twenty-one. I decided it would be twenty-one for me. I was almost finished with university, when my father suggested I visit my grandparents in St. Ann, Jamaica, "To get a different perspective on life." They lived outside Ocho Rios in a newly developed scheme called Rio Nuevo. It was a nice place on an ample amount of land, which they made use of by planting all kinds of fruits and vegetables.

When Paul came to pick me up from the airport, I was sorry I hadn't asked for an extension on my ticket. I wasn't ready to go back to Canada.

"So, how was it?" I came back on a Saturday afternoon. The roads were less busy, so Paul just sped along.

"In a word, it was almost paradise." I transported myself backwards in time.

"Bliss. That's a big compliment to the place and hard to find."

"It's hard to know where to begin. The music is so infectious. There is a music festival or live show almost every day."

"My iPod could use some new tracks. Did you bring any back?" He seemed to have suddenly remembered the car radio and turned it on.

"Of course. I couldn't resist. And the bloody food—it's indescribable. It's like they inject the seasoning into it. I must have gained a couple pounds because I gorged myself on absolutely everything." There was a slight bulge at my stomach, evidence of the edible delight. I would have to work it off with repeated crunches.

"Is it anything like the Caribbean food we get here?" he asked, pressing the scan button to find a suitable station.

"A little bit, but everything there is heightened: heightened flavours, fresher. It's almost like your tongue is brand new and has gained additional senses."

As I spoke, I could taste the jerk, the ackee and saltfish, and all the other food I had pigged out on over the past weeks.

"Did you go to the beach?"

"Like I could go to Jamaica and not go to the beach. Where my grandparents live, just outside Ocho Rios, I woke up and saw the sea every morning. Can you imagine that? I also went to a real river."

"River, sea—what's the difference?"

"Clearer water, huge rocks, different ebb and flow. It's smaller and has more life. No sand, just land."

"Wow, I envy you."

"You could go, you know."

"I have nobody in that exotic place of yours."

"I meant with me, the next time I go."

We slipped onto the 427 and passed a huge billboard displaying a huge truck overpowering and conquering a mountain. If you want to dominate all kinds of terrain, you have to get that truck. Who comes up with all these invincible vehicles?

"So—Ocho Rios, what's that like?"

"Quaint. It's like Kitchener but with a constant feeling of warmth. It has a pulse."

"So it's small, then."

"Yea, it's small. There's a clock that's the centre of everything in the town. You can run around it in fifteen minutes. But there's a largeness about the place too. It's like it's small, but the people there can still do anything. You hear it in the music; it just transports you to another place. You gotta go to know."

"Cool. So how are your grandparents?" He had found a station he liked, and now his fingers repeatedly tapped the steering wheel.

"Like regular grandparents. They know that you have grown up, but every time they see you, they act surprised at how tall you are. They fuss over you too. They are fantastic."

"So it was all good?"

I paused. It was mostly good. But every place on earth has its flaws.

"One of my grandparents' neighbours has a male dog that does a lot of running around."

"You mean he won't sit still, or do you mean he fucks around?"

"The latter."

"That's what dogs do, isn't it?"

"Perhaps, but people don't like a yard filled with unwanted dogs, especially not mongrels."

"People don't like this, and they don't like that, but that doesn't change what is."

"That's where you're wrong. People will find ways, especially if they care about something enough. Apparently these dogs can be very destructive when they are attempting to get near their females, tearing down fences and enclosures. People are very particular about their fences. This guy came over with a huge thing that looked like a scissors, and he split the dog's sack right in half; the balls fell right out. There was no anaesthetic. They just put some ashes on it. It was like something from another century. I have never heard such howling and screaming all my life. The dog was running around in circles, sometimes running for the fences but not seeing where the hell he was going."

"Shit, pain will do that to you."

One of Paul's hands dropped from tapping of the wheel and headed for his nether regions. It lingered there for some time.

"And the dog sat still for this?"

"It's hard to move or run when you're tied up."

"Wasn't there bleeding?"

"I don't know for sure, but apparently the ashes helped. It's supposed to be an antiseptic. I didn't get that close. A dog like that, one that just lost its balls, is a mad dog, I imagine. That's no place for me to stand around."

"Ashes, huh, that's appropriate. Ashes to ashes, dust to dust. After something like that, it's death of a sort. So what, they couldn't afford a vet?"

"Sometimes it's not about the money. It's a tradition, just something they do."

"Shit, you don't find that practise unpleasant?"

"I felt like my own fucking balls were on fire that day, and the wind-whistling wailing just went on and on. I felt like the yelping actually sapped my energy. I left and went into the town, and when I came back, the racket was still going on. I was relieved when it all just turned into a whimper."

"I think that's when the demoralized dog just gave up and thought, 'Shit, they cut right into my balls; I may as well give up.'"

"I thought that's when the pain began to go away."

"Yea, right. Like somebody is going to cut your little pouch open, rip out your marbles, and the pain would cease anytime soon."

Paul's index and middle fingers made a makeshift scissors, cutting away over the steering wheel. His fingers were small, though. The implement used on the dog had been much bigger.

"You have a point."

"So what about the girls?"

"You would love Jamaica."

We zipped along the highway, talking about music, food, and a neutered dog, and I thought about my father and his advice to gain other perspectives. I had learnt that opening up to new foods could put a whole different taste in your mouth, that the kind of music you listened to could affect your very soul. I also saw there was no difference between dogs and men when it came to losing their balls. The results were just the same: a lot of howling and running into closed gates.

7 April 2006

I did marry the kind of woman my father had suggested. I don't know if it was deliberate or accidental. Debbie believed in me and told me, "John, you can do this; John, you can do that." But I didn't follow through on my father's recommendations. My wife's suggestions only served to fuel my insecurities. It sounds stupid, I know. Other people are inspired when somebody who loves them prods them on, but I am a different species. We were the same age, but she had already done a first degree in mass communications and a master's degree in communications, so I had a wife who wrote everyday and knew how to communicate effectively. I also had a wife who wanted the best for me.

"John," she would say, "why don't you do your master's degree in psychology now? You've got some cash; you can do it part-time, so you don't have to leave your job if that's a concern. It would be another goal that you could pursue. I'm sure it could be worked out to a happy medium."

"I have enough on my plate as it is. I don't know why you want me to use up my free time."

"You know, John, I don't know why everything I say to you must be met with such staunch resistance. It's almost as if anything I can say will be opposed and twisted in a very unsavoury way. What is it with you? Can't you even listen to a suggestion, process it, and then make a rational judgement?"

"So you're saying I'm being irrational?"

"I'm saying I can't talk to you at all. There is this big barrier just like in other aspects of this marriage."

"I thought we were talking about doing a master's degree in psychology."

"I am talking about a general lack of willingness on your part to be anything else other than the way you are now—negative and unreachable."

"Is this a line from an article you wrote recently? Because I have no idea what you're talking about. I can't deal with this crap."

"Of course not—to deal with this crap would mean letting yourself go and participating in something. That wouldn't be you, would it, John? This conversation came about because I asked you about doing a degree. Do you see something wrong here?"

"Yea, I see you getting on my case."

When Maya told me to write, and I asked her what to write about, one of the things she said to write down was any conversation I could remember that was significant. I'm writing down even the ones that don't seem so important because I'm learning day by day that words hold a certain power, one I never knew they had. At school we heard, "Sticks and stones can hurt my bones, but words can never hurt me." We also said, "Word is wind," usually to people who tried to hurt us with them. But if word was wind, it was like a strong gust that could blow and uproot even the strongest trees. They could certainly hurt our bones.

Everything I utter says something about me, and everything I hear has an impact on me. Perhaps most important are the words I use to myself. I know for sure that this psycholinguistics or language of the mind could work for me, especially in building a creative way for me to move forward. These are the things I write in my logs every day. This is what I tell my patients daily, but I can't use it in my own life. If I know it, why can't I use it?

10 April 2006

I'm always trying to build a relationship of trust with my clients. I want to see them progress. If they don't, what's the point? It would mean I'm not doing my job. Of course, it takes lots of effort. I find some of their resistance frustrating, but everyone has to make his or her own decisions. I try to take care of my frustrations by having lunch with my friends. That's what happened yesterday—eating my frustrations away. No, it's more like having my friends around me like a buffer. Paul's talk about finance and Maya's marketing strategies serve to distract me.

"You seem a bit distracted, John." Maya was picking at her garden salad, turning over green leaves with her fork.

"I'm preoccupied with going to court next week." The smell of the curry chicken, which both Paul and I had ordered, was delectable.

"Why are you going to court?"

"I am seeing a twelve-year-old boy and his mother. The boy has been having behavioural problems since his parents divorced. He wants to live with his father. I have to give testimony about his emotional state." The taste of the curry lived up to its smell; it was melt-in-your-mouth food.

"Sounds familiar. Can what you say make an impact?"

"That's got to be why they are asking him. This is good," Paul said, spitting out chicken bones and eagerly going to the next piece.

"I want to say the right things and not what I am led to say. These things can be so challenging."

The restaurant was packed, and people were waiting in the foyer to be seated. Controlling a busy restaurant downtown at lunchtime could be demanding.

"It's your profession, man; you do this all the time." Paul was partly finished, having eaten quickly, like a man who was half-starved.

"Yes, but this feels a little different."

"Sounds like you're emotionally involved. Do you see you yourself in this boy?" There she went again, examining my thoughts in detail and dissecting my words to the point where I wondered how she came up with that analysis from the simple things I said.

"No. I don't know. All I know is that ever since Debbie left me, I feel like I shouldn't be telling anybody what to do."

"You mean professionally."

"Yes."

I did a survey once where they asked about noise in a restaurant and how it impacted my overall experience. Apparently the overpowering hum and racket at some eateries could even be violating some noise abatement act. But sometimes I just wanted to eat without the analysis, and the distraction of the restaurant helped.

"Man, please, people get divorced every day. Suck it up. It's your fault for choosing that profession anyway. Giving therapy is more suited to women. They have the emotional capacity to deal with those kinds of things." Paul closed his knife and fork and leaned back in his seat.

"John, ignore what Paul just said. He's a prime example of why we hold certain opinions of men."

"I hate when she talks about me using pronouns as distance, as if I weren't sitting right here. John, I am joking, but really, it's the profession you chose."

"There's a reason he chose that profession."

Maybe I didn't know what I wanted. Maya's analysis always gave me a new angle to look at. Yet there were times when the angles she presented were too new for me.

"I don't know why I did. There is certainly no intrinsic reason I can think of."

"I chose finance because that's what I'm good at, and Maya … look at her. You can sell anything if you look good. Image is everything."

It certainly is, and my image of myself isn't good.

"I still believe that you and psychology go together."

"That's the marketing side of you talking. You're always trying to link two things together. When you figure out the reason why I am a therapist, please let me know what it is."

"Maybe that's how you keep your own sanity." She had finally given up on her leafy vegetables and allowed her fork to fall for good.

"I didn't know John was going crazy!"

"Paul, craziness is just below the surface of all of us. It's a thin line between sanity and insanity, and it takes just a bit to push us over sometimes. Of course, some of us are a bit stronger, but in the end, we all have limits to what we can bear. I learnt that because of my job, but I am sure of it because of my own inadequacies."

"We are all inadequate, man, but that's no reason to go off the deep end. Shortcomings are common place; it's part of everyday living."

"You're right, but there are different levels of inadequacies."

"John, let's stop talking about inadequacies. Let's focus on something you're good at—like your job. There's no need to worry about going to court. Why? Because you have done this before. Because you know the case and will speak to what you know. After that, it's out of your hands. Do your part, and then let it go. Don't take on the world; just do your little part, and the rest will fall into place."

I finished my lunch, listening to the clanging of plates and the rattling of utensils in the background and wondering about letting go. How do I let go of everything that is hanging up my life, when all I know how to do is hang on for dear life?

13 April 2006

I woke this morning in cold sweat from dreams I could have escaped sooner. In the darkness of the apartment, I lay in bed and listened to silence and emptiness. I saw in my mind's eye every space that's empty because the pieces of furniture are gone, every circled impression where a Michael Layne vase once stood. Debbie loved ceramic art, and she especially loved Layne's work. I don't see myself replacing anything she took with her. What's the point? I don't need end tables or coffee tables with lifestyle magazines laid out on top of them. I have absolutely no time to obtain vases of varying sizes and colours to accentuate this and that in the living room and the patio. And drapes—who has time to colour coordinate?

I have a bed to sleep in. I have a 50" flat-screen TV to watch sports and movies, and I have a place to sit in front of it. Now I have a ponytail palm that looks like a huge onion with lots of long, skinny leaves that resemble party trimmings. The lady in the plant shop told me the palm would reach about three feet indoors, but she also said that when grown outdoors in a warm climate, it could easily reach twenty feet tall. What a big difference environment and conditions can make. I wonder about my present surroundings and why we bought a three bedroom apartment.

We never discussed having children; I guess it was assumed, like she assumed I was a whole person. We didn't discuss a lot of things. So now I am in one room with only the sound of my own voice to come back to me. All empty rooms with echoes of the past—echoes of failures, of things left unsaid and undone, of things that might never be. The only things I have are dreams and memories, and sometimes they are both wrapped up in one.

I called Maya at five-thirty in the morning.

"You know, John, it's a good thing I'm single. Do you think I keep up my beauty from a lack of sleep?"

"Forgive my inconsideration, but I need a listening ear. Kicking your controlling boyfriend to the curb was my gain."

"Mine too. What is so urgent at this hour of the morning?"

"Dreams."

"And you think I can interpret them?"

"I don't know whether you can, but I need to get them out in the air. I dreamt I went to court and answered the questions that were put to me, but in the end the little boy wasn't allowed to live with either his father or mother. He was sent to a boys' home run by the government."

I imagined I could hear Maya's brain starting up like a machine that had been left on idle but now had a reason to warm up.

"That's a very sad dream. You know how terrible these government-run institutions can be. That's what the media would have us believe anyway. I've seen some horror stories in the news, and I really have to wonder how accurate those stories are. Seriously though, I think it's just a manifestation of your worse fears."

"It's not even logical. The boy has perfectly decent parents, so there is no question of him ever going to a home."

"When were dreams ever logical? They are the metaphors of our subconscious. They are intriguing because they are like parables to be figured out. When your parents split up, which one did you want to live with?"

"I don't know. What does this have to do with me?"

"Maybe nothing; maybe something. Maybe the state-run facility isn't such a terrible place after all. Maybe it's that middle ground you keep wanting."

"It sounds like you're trying to market yet another idea to me. It's minutes to six, and I have some heavy cases in front of me, so let's keep this simple. This has to do with one of my cases, not me."

"All right, I am going to pretend that you didn't just wake me up to seek my input. And I will also play along and pretend this has nothing to do with you."

"Thanks for your understanding. I also dreamt I was in Kingston by my father's place. There's a little water place not far from where he lived. It's not the smoothest part, not beachy; in fact, it's rocky, but that's part of the charm and fun of the place. I used to play there a lot as a boy. I have fun memories of that place. But last night, I was drowning in it, and when I came up the third time, you and Debbie were reaching for me, calling out my name and telling me to take your outstretched hands. And all the time I was struggling to come up, I could see my mother's face at the bottom of the river. The thing is the face was so inviting and familiar that I didn't know what to do."

"So did you take it?"

"Take what?"

"The outstretched hands."

"That's when I woke up, drenched in sweat."

"Just like you to leave a woman hanging."

"It's not deliberate. I can't seem to help myself."

"How long are you going to use that? Don't say it's because you don't know. I don't know what it means for sure, but I want to believe that it's very simple. The outstretched hands are going to save you. I'm flattered that I was on the bank giving you a hand. It's funny, but your wife was there too, and I think that's significant. The face at the bottom of the river is inviting you to drown—or so you think. I don't know if this is literally or figuratively. This is something you need to figure out on your own. I don't believe Aunt Martha was trying to drown you. I think you have a skewed perspective, and it's all you and no one else. John, one thing I know is that it's easy to die or drown. You don't have to do a damn thing. Don't swim, just sink. It's much harder to live because it takes effort. Just reach for the hands and lift yourself out of the water."

Maybe my perspective was indeed skewed, but the dream had been so real I was drenched when I woke up. I was also thankful that I hadn't drowned.

"Why do you think it was Kingston?"

"Because it's a place you felt safe, protected, and free. I don't know."

"If that is true, why would I be drowning there?"

"Subconsciously, do you want to surface? Does that sound logical?"

"It sounds like something I want to hold onto."

"While you are holding onto that, you might want to find out what Debbie was doing, standing on a riverbank in Kingston trying to save you. Have you ever taken her there?"

"No. We always meant to go, and my father was always asking when we were coming, but it never happened."

"Pity. Now let me go back to bed."

She made sense, as she usually does. I just wonder what I am going to do with all the logic she showed me. Maybe I should go to Kingston and see if I can find some of this safety, protection, and freedom that supposedly I have there. It really wouldn't cost me anything but time. That's another thing I have.

I lay back in bed with the time I had and thought about my patients—the boy and his mother—and then I thought about the dream, Kingston, and my father. At the time of my parents' divorce, I was torn between my father and my mother, but I wasn't given a choice. By the time I was seven, I didn't want him to touch me because of that same feeling of powerlessness. As soon as he left, she started clearing the house of things she claimed were worthless and which took up more space than she could afford. For every piece she cleared out, she found some piece of art for its replacement—some kind of bird made from a bike's gas tank, a man made from exhaust pipes, a guitar-playing man made from unidentifiable scraps of rusty machinery.

It was a case of any media to create an experience. I didn't know why the space in our home had to be used this way. So my father had to leave, but this grotesque contraption of somebody's garish imagination got to live with us? She seemed enthralled by their very presence. Her eyes looked at the pieces with love. Her long fingers caressed their contours and intertwined themselves in the patchworks of the abstractions in languid dances.

"Why did he have to leave?" I asked my mother, disturbing her rhythm, maybe bringing her mind back from wherever it had gone. She pulled away slowly and sighed, as if it was a pain to talk about something she had already cleared away.

"It's hard to explain to a boy of seven, but your father needed his space, and I needed mine. In time, you'll know all about spaces. We decided to give each other that, for our sakes and for yours. That's love too."

I didn't understand how they had made that decision on my behalf, and I didn't understand that kind of love, but I took it and filed it away somewhere below the surface of my mind. Love to me at the time was attachment, and all that was taking place was disentanglement. Love was the way she was touching her art, appending herself and becoming available to it.

"What about me?"

"What about you?" She held my face, her thumbs brushing my cheeks. I wondered if anything metallic would rub off on my face. I wondered if she saw me as one of her pieces. Well, she loved those pieces, so what could be so wrong if I was the centrepiece, having overall importance? "You get to stay with me. We get to take care of each other."

"Who'll take care of Poppy?"

"Don't worry—he'll be fine. He's happy, and I'm happy."

I wasn't sure if she meant that I should be happy too. I had never really thought about their happiness before. I knew about mine. I knew that the two of them were a part of my everyday habits. If *they weren't happy, maybe they were a bad habit, but I needed their relationship to be fixed—whether it was a good repair job or not.*

"*Boys need to take care of their mothers. Will you take care of me?*"

It was a bone she threw me, the opportunity to think I could take care of her. That would sidestep my sadness about my mother and father living in two separate places, sidestep my own irritation when I was sure they got to express theirs with each other before the pretence of amicability, and sidestep the fact that I would be forced to visit my father in a completely different city.

"*Yes.*" *What else could I have said? It was true too. I wanted to take care of her. I thought I could make a collage out of all the severed parts that had been left behind.*

"*That's my boy.*"

That's when she promised me British Columbia.

17 April 2006

My mother called to say she had something to give me. She wouldn't say what; it was to be a surprise. I couldn't imagine what it might be, maybe a contemplative, enigmatic piece of twisted steel constructed into art for my empty, hollow apartment. Some steel would take up space, I suppose. Perhaps if I stared at it long enough, it would appeal to my "sensory perception." Those are the kinds of phrases she uses. I went to the house that had been my home once upon a time and was greeted by the usual puff of smoke.

"They say as soon as you quit smoking, you add another couple years to your life." I sat on the settee and watched her circling the living room. She is always restless. I glanced up the stairs, almost expecting someone to come down them, but they were empty.

"I am almost sixty years old, and I've been smoking from my teenage years. If I quit now, I would certainly die."

"Have you ever thought about lung cancer?"

"We all have to die some way, and it doesn't make any difference how we go out. I am not craving any additional years. What would I do with them, anyway?"

I should have told her that she might kill me with her self-destructive behaviour, but why bother? She would probably just say that secondhand smoke is good for her immune system. As irrational and illogical as that sounds, she has her belief system.

"So what's this big surprise?"

"I've decided to hand over a precious family legacy to you. That chair over there that first you loved and then you hated—it's yours. So if I suddenly fall prey to the lung cancer you keep telling me about, I bequeath this to you."

I leaned back in the settee and closed my eyes, wondering why this was happening to me. Will this saga never end? That bloody chair has now come around full circle.

"Who else do you have to leave things to—the Art Society of Toronto?"

"The Art Society could certainly benefit from a few pieces, but this is a family affair."

She continued walking around the room, touching objects wrapped up in wads of brown paper. I suspected they were pieces of her art; they are the only things she ever touches that way.

"I don't understand why you feel the need to give me this now." I stood up from the settee, ready to leave.

"Well, if you want to give someone something, there's no time like the present. Plus, it's in the way."

"There it is. I don't know why I'm always some kind of receptacle for your refuse."

"I'm giving you one chair, a family heirloom at that, and you're saying I'm giving you junk? Either you are very unappreciative and don't know the value of family traditions, or you're just tired from all the problems you have closed up in files and locked in those grey government drawers. I am going to attribute it to the latter."

At fifty-eight, my mother has hair as grey as the smoke that swirls around her head, with only streaks of black. It gives her the distinguished look of a seasoned gallery owner, someone who knows how to make people think revolutionary art should be mainstream. She has that authoritative tone too, the one curators use when they know what they are talking about, and I was hearing it now.

"My closed files are the least of my problems. There are other things that make me tired. But you wouldn't know about that."

"So, will you be taking it with you this evening? I have just acquired two Sandra Spences, and I have a lovely piece by Norval Edwards that could go in that space. It is one of those pieces that stops viewers in their tracks and makes them ask questions. The man is a genius. The things he can do with metal are truly groundbreaking. He's before his time."

And I want to be just a typical man living in this time. I suppose that is what all men want. I contemplated refusing the object flat out. After all, why should I take something that I didn't want?

In the end, I loaded up the object I most associated with my mother's upper-middle-class prostitution and thought about her audacity in giving it to me. Maybe it is fitting that it has been bestowed upon me; maybe that chair can save me where other things have not. I just have to figure out how.

After a while, I allowed the garden to fall into disrepair. When disorder is perceived all around, nothing stays in order; the need to upkeep is forsaken. There is only entanglement, bushes, and a vague sense that something once groomed, cultivated, and preserved had been there. I don't even know if it was a conscious decision, or if over time it just fell along the wayside as a natural process of slow death and decline. I just lost interest in the futility of it all.

My mother said nothing about the garden. I guess she just assumed that death was a natural process in life. Sometimes her silences were just as infuriating as her words, if not more so. With all the time I had spend building it and all the time I spent outdoors watching the entire process, she could have said something. But I could always rely on Aunt Daphne to notice and comment on things. When she came for tea with my mother, I would observe them talking.

They were both tall, dark, beautiful women, commanding with their presence. The older one, the educator of children; the other, hawker of innovative art. Sometimes I wondered what they talked about when they were alone.

"I turn my back for a second, and things fall apart. Where's the garden, John?"

I shrugged my shoulders, as if to say things happened, and one of those things was a forsaken garden. We were on the patio at the back of the house, which led to where the garden was. Maya was there too. She could have been twelve at the time, but I cannot recall. I can remember her being as skinny as a pencil, the way girls her age are thin. Whenever she bothered me, I would tell her I would blow her away, and no one would find her because she would be in another country.

"Shrugging is the body language of the unenthusiastic, and I know that you are not that." Aunt Daphne looked at me the way I imagined she looked at the students in her class, daring them to give her an appropriate answer.

"I am not unenthusiastic; I am just not interested anymore."

"All good things must come to an end. He's just outgrown butterflies and gardens." My mother looked outside, as if she was glad I had finally grown up. Maybe that's what she wanted to believe, but that would be her version of growing up.

"I suppose these things do happen, but he was so passionate."

"So what are you interested in now, John?" Maya and I stood facing each other by the door. Even then, she was asking me tough questions.

"Why do you want to know?"

"Because I am interested," she replied.

"Leave him alone," Aunt Daphne told Maya. "So, John, you are not engaged anymore, but I'll miss seeing it. It was so lush and colourful here. It was a joy to just sit here and watch. I suppose it's still lush but in a knotted sort of way."

"Sorry, Aunt Daph, if I had known you liked it so much, I might have made the effort to stay interested."

"What was it? You weren't getting the results you wanted? Results increase fascination, I know. Was it that repulsive stage that finally got to you?"

"No. I became accustomed to that."

"Customary unpleasantness, hmmm." She seemed to understand, but I was sure we were thinking about two different things.

They retired for their customary tea. Through the pane of the glass, we could see them from the patio. My mother poured the tea from the kettle, one of those with a long spout. The steam rose, snaking and evaporating in the air, a tall tale without legs to stand on. Maya trailed behind me.

"So, are you going to take up a new hobby?"

"Maybe."

Aunt Daphne smiled and gesticulated, sitting forward and touching her sister's legs from time to time, making a point in their conversation. Her black curls shone and dangled, complementing her motions. My mother's hair was up in one of her customary curator buns, an impressive mixture of salt with a dash of pepper. It was what I called her gallery hairstyle, and I rarely saw her wear it any other way. It gave her a reserved look. I didn't mind it selling art, but I didn't want to see it at home.

"Why maybe? Don't you know what you're going to do?"

"Why do I have to do anything at all, and why are you bugging me?"

I heard the sounds of cups against saucers and thought about how my mother tried hard not to smoke when my aunt was around. Aunt Daphne should move in. Who knew what other things she could accomplish?

"Aunt Martha says you have butterflies in your head, and Mom says you are totally absorbed in your projects, as she wishes we all were. So I would say you need something to fill the void."

I looked at my skinny cousin, her black hair in ponytails, and wondered what she knew about voids. Did she mean a general emptiness, or did she know about the abysmal state of nothingness?

22 April 2006

Friday night. Spadina Avenue again. DJ Squeeze was at club Locust, and the rave would be on. Paul was chasing skirts, and Maya had to spend time with her girls. I didn't drive to the club because I intended to drink. I am a responsible imbiber who takes the taxi when there is no designated driver to get me home. I kid myself that I am socially accountable in some ways, but the last thing I want to do is appear as a reenactment in a MADD ad. It wouldn't be good for my professional reputation, and it would just not be a good thing overall.

The club was rocking in high energy, and out of nowhere some fool accused me of staring at his woman, as if we didn't live in a democracy where people are allowed to look. In any case, I didn't even see his woman; ask me what she looked like, and I couldn't tell you. But there is only one place to go when two men boosted up with alcohol have a problem to settle. Here I was in yet another drama, someone who had never had a bar fight until he was twenty-eight. Now I have two under my belt. It was a slugfest where my rage came pouring out, and I just wanted to punch the shit face in front of me into oblivion. It didn't get any better when the cops got there. When I was hauled outside and placed in the back of a cruiser, I still had some fight and bravado left in me. At Forty-Two Division, they threw me in a cell to cool off. That's what the uniforms said too: "Go cool off in there, buddy." They wouldn't let me leave until someone responsible came to collect me, as if I were a wayward child who had done some wrong at school. I guess they meant anybody who was sober and who was not involved in foolish boxing matches.

A sober and bleary-eyed Maya came to get me, and for her I felt remorse because once again I had taken her out of bed and out of her way. Who wanted to drive from the west end of the city to the centre for no good reason?

"Your face is going to need some looking after, maybe stitches too," she yawned.

"Please, so is the other guy's. He's probably going to need to stay in bed for the next couple days." I waved my hands away as if to say it was nothing.

"I see through all of this you still have a sense of humour. It's a good thing the police do too. I'm beginning to sound like a broken record, but you've got to stop this. And you know what? I have earned the right to be this way. Every time you get into one of these unfortunate situations, you call me. Why don't you call Paul or some other person?"

"He probably wouldn't hear a drum in his ear, much less a call from me. I love you for coming."

"What was it this time?"

"Self defence."

"Right. Wasn't that the case last time?"

"I guess I must have punch bag written all over my face."

"No, as I told you last time, the sickly smell of trouble and easy pickings are what is written all over you."

"If a guy wants to punch the lights out of me, what should I do? Should I just say go ahead? Should I turn the other cheek? That kind of invitation for additional abuse is highly overrated.

King James just threw that one in there. Seventy times seven—are you kidding me?"

I could hear iron doors slamming behind me in the distance.

"Listen. What happened to you last night was a mixture of drinks, testosterone, and the issues you have in your head. It doesn't take much to tick you off in a bar, so stop this nonsense about defence. The only person you need protection against is yourself. You are at the mercies of your very self."

"So you're going to lecture me. I have a righteous headache, my face is all torn up, and you're going to add to the pain. I didn't know you were a sadist."

"Ah, poor baby. If anybody is sadistic, it's you because of the pain you inflict on yourself."

Her index finger wagged at me, a schoolteacher chastising a child.

"Stop going to bars, or just stop going to them alone. These fights or bar brawls are not you. What is it, some outward expression of your inner demons? Be the refined person you are. Stay home, listen to music, and drink your juice, and if you want to pick fights, call your mother."

"Must you bring her into everything that comes up?"

"Must you?" She pointed an accusatory finger at me. "Suppose you were charged? They could have charged your black ass just because you're being stupid. This out-of-control behaviour could cost you your freedom and your integrity. Are you looking for a record? Jesus, I could slap some sense into you sometimes. Guilty by stupidity."

"You would be so sadistic to slap this beaten-up face?"

She sighed helplessly, as if there were nothing more she could do for me. Maybe there wasn't. She couldn't do more for me than I could do for myself.

By the time I got home, it was five in the morning, and I was so wound up that I couldn't go to sleep. I paced from room to room. And there was that bleeding chair right where I had left it. Well, where else did I expect it to be? It had legs, but it could not walk. It was a pity because if it could walk, maybe it would voluntarily take a permanent hike from my home. Where do you put something you don't want to see? I chose a room I didn't go into very often, but I knew the chair was there. I saw it in my mind's eye, like I saw all the furnishings that were no longer there.

At first, I was disoriented by the gaps in the settings, sometimes almost tripping over the unexpected room that was available, sometimes losing my breath because I knew what was there and what it represented. It wasn't the missing tables, chairs, paintings, racks for holding things in; all the room just represented my failures and shortcomings. But then it became familiar—even space becomes familiar if you spend enough time with it. Since I have all this space, I might as well put a positive spin on it. My home is now spacious, like the galleries I visit from time to time. The ones I wander into trying to find breathing room. I have become a minimalist by default. My wife has cleared her stuff out, and I am content to live with emptiness. The more I think about the chair, the more I feel my chest tighten and my heart race. Hell, it feels like an oncoming heart attack.

I must have dozed off a bit because I jumped up, and it was the first thing I thought of. So I had gone to sleep with it and woken up to it, as if it were an intriguing lover who wouldn't leave my mind. And like a lover's touch, it has presence and power, and like magnet it draws me into that room to look at it. Fatal attraction. How many grown men operate this way—falling prey to a goddamn chair or to another inanimate object? It is pitiful and laughable.

I inspected it thoroughly. Did it have screws or was it held together by strong adhesive? Oh yea, it was screws. Flat-head or round-head screws. Didn't matter, anyway. Saturday morning, instead of making up for the sleep I had missed, robbed when I had sat in a jail cell waiting for my release, I sat in the middle of an empty room with an aged chair. History was in that chair, perhaps interesting stories of my antecedents. But there was also authority in this chair, and I wanted to break and challenge it. My boxers were my only clothing, Toronto's cold was on, but all I felt was heat steaming through the walls of the house and through every pore of my body, sort of like the way I thought male menopause would feel at the ripe old age of twenty-eight.

Somehow I was led to get my tool kit. I started at the top. The first piece came rattling off with a sweet clang—the sounds of wood hitting floor, bouncing off the four walls. Then came the spines in the middle, with more delightful sounds. The Phillips was a friend helping me to exorcise my ghosts. With every piece that fell, something almost orgasmic and unnameable escaped me. The seat itself fell with a deep thud, but to me, it was still a whole seat, and so I took my time sawing it into unrecognizable, harmless strips with the power saw I had bought at Canadian Tire. The sweet drone of the saw humming was music to my ears. The four legs took care of themselves. The rocking parts at the base were strange to look at, standing alone with nothing on top to rock. They looked a bit like boomerangs, but I was hoping that they and all that they represented would not come back to me.

Once I had finished dismantling of the rocking chair, with sweat running down my face and neck and onto the floor like tears, I stretched out on the floor and breathed. Looking at the weird assemblage of wood scattered all about me, I wondered whether I should burn it or simply leave it out for Toronto's always-tardy garbage trucks. Maybe I should return it to my mother and tell her to ask one of the artists she represented to make something completely new out of the grand mess. Maybe one of them could do an installation and call it *Lost* or *Found*.

That was just a fanciful idea because a large part of me wants ashes. I want a certain disintegration from which that chair could never be recovered. If I lived in a house, I would have gone into to the backyard and burned them, but in a condo complex, you can't just get up and start a fire at leisure—unless you want the police on your doorsteps, and I have seen enough of the police to last me for a while. The next time, the men in blue might not be so understanding; bar brawls and arson are not the same. I have time, though, so for now I am content to lay in the middle of this splendid disarray of cedar wood.

27 April 2006

My court appearance came and went. I didn't know if I should have been neutrally passive or passionately convicted. In the end, all I did was tell the truth as I knew it. The rest was up to the court, out of my hands. I haven't decided whether I am going to go back to Kingston, but it is always looming in the background, like a distant lighthouse beckoning to a ship lost in choppy waters. Maybe that isn't a fair description. The city of Kingston isn't much of a drive from where I live, only two-and-a-half-hours at most, so much closer than the island of my grandparents. But what I would accomplish by going isn't so clear to me.

By the time I left the courthouse, my day was done. Courthouses and their procedures take time, sometimes with no definite conclusion. I had just enough time in the afternoon to go to a travelling exhibition at a gallery downtown on Queen West that had a show on the Tainos. It was making its way around North America, telling a dark tale of loss. Maya's company had the account to market this particular exhibition, so of course, she dragged me along. It was mainly artefacts and pictures of artefacts. The Tainos, the Indians who initially inhabited the Caribbean, were long dead. They were trampled by the Spaniards, with their big guns, huge horses, and alien culture. There exhibition contained the wooden gods they once worshipped, the stools they once sat on, and lots of the exquisite pottery they once made. It was a demonstration of unbelievable durability that such beautiful things could survive such terrible ordeals. These were dug up by archaeologists, not unlike the students I went to university with, students who always wanted to make a great find and who were willing to travel all over the world to find one.

"I just love the smell of galleries," Maya said. "They smell like stories of a past life."

I knew just what she meant. There's a certain smell that galleries—and especially museums—tend to have. They smell old and dusty, like antiques, and the fragrance always transports me back to the time of the displays. But this exhibit smelled somehow ... grimmer, more dead than the usual mustiness, so I told her, "Well, this exhibition reeks of death and destruction."

"Well, there is that, but there is culture too. We can see how they lived their lives; you know what they did from day to day. So—how was court today?'

I turned from a variety of cracked pottery.

"It's over. Actually, it wasn't bad. I said what I knew, and that was that."

"See, you were worried for nothing. Oh, look at that stool—isn't it interesting and gorgeous?"

I looked at the stool she pointed at. It was interesting. I wondered if it was fragile, since it had been made so long ago, or whether they put some sort of product on it to keep it from falling apart. Would anybody be able to sit on it now? I knew they had restoration and preservation in terms of paintings, so they must have it for artefacts too. They would not survive for long without some kind of preservative.

"I don't know if I was worried, or if I just felt unworthy."

"Unworthy?"

"You know, of treating people and giving expert opinion."

"So we are back down this road again?"

"Frankly, we never left. I am just barely holding myself together."

"You know, John, I never want to be giving anybody advice on anything as it relates to personal battles. All I know is how to develop and sell an image. I have my own shit, like maybe how I should stop smoking. The thing is, I really don't want to because I don't see a bloody thing wrong with it."

"How to stop smoking? Or how to reconcile doing marijuana in Bible leaves? It's not like you are a habitual smoker of cigarettes."

The place smelled like artefacts too. Not that I knew exactly how they were supposed to smell; it just had the odour of antiquity.

"You enjoyed that story to the max. I did that once, but you are going to hang onto it forever. It's not me; it's just something I did long ago. Anyway, marijuana is a religious substance. It's meditative."

"Sure, but you are not Rastafarian. Getting high is not a religion."

"It might not be, but it would be a good one. Don't they talk about getting high on God? As I was saying about selling an image, that's what I do for a living, but you have been selling an image too. And you know that an image is just that—an image; it's not necessarily you. You are not a bar fighter. You are neither cold nor distant. I could go on and on about who you are *not*. It's like you are outside of your own true self. I know you. You are compassionate, caring, and a good man. That's the John I know. But you have sucked up some stuff from long ago that you project as yourself to other people, and it's killing you. Maybe that's why you lost your wife. She doesn't know the man I know. Why are you laughing?"

"I am standing in a gallery, looking at the artefacts left behind by the Taino Indians, who were decimated by another people's culture."

"Why is that funny?"

"Because it's like me, being destroyed by someone else's views of the world. How funny is that?"

But is what I said really true? Our own thoughts have a way of going out into the universe and then coming back like a boomerang to make us who we are.

"I don't know about funny, but there is one difference: You aren't dead. There is still time to get back to being John, and you can create your own views. I am sure you have your own beliefs. That poster over there is about Taino retentions—you know, the artefacts they left behind. They left their mark on their conquerors and on the places where they lived. And that's really what this exhibition is about, not the trampling and destruction, but the retentions."

"That's really precious, a eulogy to the dead, but I want to know why I am such a fool. How could it be that I just assimilated so much of the shit my mother spewed out? I am a man; men aren't supposed to be affected by shit like this."

The organizers of the exhibition had replicated a hut that the Taino chiefs used to inhabit. Their huts were different from those of the ordinary people, and yet the hierarchy had not saved them from annihilation.

"You are just human like the rest of us. Don't get sucked into the gender stereotypes. This guy at work—he started trembling uncontrollably and couldn't stop. He looked as if he was having a nervous breakdown. It turns out, his father died, and he didn't cry or do any of the stuff that people do to mourn when someone they loved passes on. What, men don't feel stuff? Who isn't influenced by the hand that holds us to the bosom? We are our mother's children."

"I am my father's child too."

"Sure, but did he feed you milk from his breast?" She touched her breasts in demonstration. "Look at the picture of the canoes they used to use. They built them themselves, you know. Look at the craftsmanship."

It was a work of art and certainly better than the bent metal my mother called art. Pity they hadn't used the canoes to escape the grappling hold of destruction. Another missed opportunity. We walked past a sign that told us the Tainos were once mistakenly called the Arawak Indians because they had a similar look and a similar culture. Because of this, the information on the Tainos had to be revised. The pottery had distinctive traits that provided vital clues in differentiating the two. Maybe I should revisit my past and my perceptions. Resembling something and being that something might be two different things.

"So—what about your chair?"

"That piece of crap was never mine; it was the bane of my existence. It belongs in the archives of history, perhaps in a place like this. It's not a chair anymore, remember?"

"I meant, what are you going to do with it?'

"I haven't decided, but I love to think of how dismantled it is and how I have the power to do whatever I want with it. Maybe I'll take the various pieces to Kingston with me."

When are you going?"

I thought I was finished with pointed questions for the day. There was yet another poster, this one with the Taino gods made to resemble animals and birds. The people who put the exhibition together had used words like *zoomorphic* and *avian*, but I preferred the simpler explanation of someone unschooled in that jargon.

"I've not decided yet."

There were so many birdlike objects, it felt as if I were in an aviary. The experts surmised this had to do with the Tainos' constant preoccupation with flight as a means of escape. I guessed they were let down by their gods, who didn't help them find a way out.

"You are undecided about a lot of things."

"The earth wasn't built in a day. Remember, God took almost a week to do it, and on the seventh day, he rested."

"Yes, but he was building an entire universe."

I am just trying to build my life, at least the kind of life I want, and that is my universe. How hard can that be, and how long will that take?

1 May 2006

A new day and a new month. I have been writing down my past conversations, my present conversations, and my thoughts for three whole months. This is an accomplishment. I am analysing this journal like the notes I take on my patients, but self-analysis is a challenge. As I write, I hear the clock ticking, and in this semi-empty domicile, the sound is dominant. It's all I can hear—time slipping away, and me trying not to slip away with it. Or, I should say, I am trying to find myself before I lose too much time. Nobody told me about this stuff. The only thing I know is that I was born a male, and that made me ready for the world. The clock is always ticking somewhere; maybe I shouldn't analyse too much into it.

I've never confronted my mother outright about the men she saw—not in a way that would bring about a huge fight of culmination. We talk around it. We are both like shadowboxers in that regard. Or maybe it was I who was the shadowboxer. Sure, I have thrown an ashtray in anger, and I have tried to spoil her rendezvous in different ways, but I have never asked her the big questions. I always thought that if I were patient, all her affairs would end, but that never happened. There were just different men at different times. By the time it was time to go to university, I was ready to escape. Living on campus was never something that appealed to me; it wasn't even necessary.

Forest Hill was just a short drive from the school, and the comfort and the amenities of my own home were things to consider. Yet life away from my mother sounded good. She had a hold on me, though. So one more time before I made my exit from home, I tried to do what I could not do for years.

"So you have decided to occupy a cell-like room and share a bathroom with fifty other people. It's a little crude and—well, oafish—but maybe it will make a man out of you, this army barracks sort of life."

"I am already a man. I was born that way, and despite your efforts to erode that, I am what I am. The only difference between campus and here is the room is bigger. The traffic going and coming is the same, if you want to talk about unsophisticated living."

"Your so-called sarcasm amuses me, and it does not become you. The thing with sarcasm is you need balls to make it come off. This is my house, and you're just a guest here, so if I want traffic, traffic there will be."

"I wasn't trying to be sarcastic; I was just stating a fact. You're a forty-eight-year-old woman. The place shouldn't be such a freeway."

We used a lot of metaphors to talk around the issues. That is what I mean by the lack of a direct confrontation. Everything had to be sanitized by a euphemism.

"You are my son. I breathed life into you, so you are in no position to lecture me or tell me how I should live my life. Ever since you were ten years old, you have been preaching to me, like your namesake John the Baptist. By now, you should see that your efforts are futile. Do you know what happened to John in the story? He lost his head, and I am afraid that very thing will happen to you. You are like a dog with a bone. You're either going to chew that bone up until there is nothing left, or it's going to frustrate you and make you mad and even rabid. I am forty-eight, and that means, as we speak, the clock is ticking towards menopause, and subsequently, I'll have to put men-on-pause, or, as you would say, stop the traffic. You can't even say the words in that pure mouth of yours. My sweet son. You are what you are, and I am what I am."

She was right. She was who she was, but who was I?

I left my mother alone in the house with her traffic. Hopefully, there would be no traffic jam and no accidents to clean up. Henry was long gone, having discovered some of her indiscretions. How could any man in his right mind stay? All he said to me was, "Your mother is too much woman for me." It was yet another euphemistic allusion, said in a way to protect me, or maybe he didn't want to offend me. I understood more than he knew. She would be too much woman for any man.

7 May 2006

The boy stayed with his mother; that was the decision of the court. Women don't lose their children unless they set them on fire. All right, that is at one extreme end of the scale; I just meant something terrible has to happen. As we all used to say at the Board of Social Work, "It was the court's decision." It's the sort of phrase like irreconcilable differences, a vague way of saying, "It's not really my fault; it just didn't work the way I wanted. Now let's wash our hands of this one and move onto the next case."

I'm not sure what could have been the best decision anyway, so I'm not making a judgement. They will still come to see me, and I will do my best to bring about some healing. He's improving with the gold-medal technique, and his mother is doing parenting and relevant life-skills training just to back up the whole process. Maybe I should pursue a master's degree. I could assist more and gain more insight through a deeper study of theory, since I don't have intuitive insight. Do males have intuition? Or do we just stumble along with our balls in our hands as compasses and hope we find our way?

Actually, that's not how my father feels. He thinks men have their own system. He calls it "mantennas." Shortly after my sixteenth birthday, I sat on a big rock with him, throwing stones into the Shrewsbury River. There aren't a lot of rivers in Canada, but there are many in Jamaica, where my father lived as a boy and that's what he named this part of the lake—Shrewsbury. Apparently, you can create any kind of space and place in your mind and go there when you want to. It can be done with physical space too; Shrewsbury was evidence of that.

"So you are almost a man now, eh?"

"I don't know. Feels the same as it did a year ago."

The stones plonked into the water, creating rippled circles before disappearing.

"Well, that's all right; the process creeps up on you. You'll feel it soon enough."

"How do you know?"

"You mean, when you are a man?"

"Yes, and how do you know stuff?"

We started a throwing competition to see who could throw the farthest, and my father always won. He had a slanted way of tossing the pebbles so that they sailed similar to the same way that one threw a Frisbee. He told me that one shouldn't use brawn all the time, and some efforts were a waste of strength. At times, success was more about finding the finesse in things. He told me not to throw against; throw with.

"You know things either by experience or intuition."

"You mean like female intuition?"

He seemed to find that funny. I had heard the term often enough from Maya and my Aunt Daphne. Of course, it was never a term my mother used because she operated by rote and not from any feminine place that I knew of. She did insist that some of her artists' pieces were from an intuitive place, a place where they contemplated, meditated, and became inspired.

"Something like that, but we have our own internal antenna."

"What's that called?"

"I call it 'mantenna.'"

"I know you made that up. I've heard of female intuition, although some of my friends say it's highly overrated. That's a real phrase, but 'mantenna'—that I don't know." I looked at the lake spread out before us, blue and simple, and I wondered how many stones it would take to fill it.

"I might have made up the word, but it works. It tells you when something is right for you, and when it's not. Make you sense a bad situation, even a bad relationship. What do you think?"

"Intuition sounds soft but sure. Your word sounds made up and without legs. It's like we have to make something up for ourselves, but we aren't even sure if it works. Females just have that thing naturally."

It would take a lot of stones and a lot of time to fill up something as vast as the lake. Maybe it couldn't be done. Attempting some things were exercises in futility.

"As interesting as that perspective is, there will come a time when that inner you, that gut feeling, will be your guide, and you'll have the 'mantenna' work. It's not an official name in the dictionary, but it is alive and will serve you well."

Paul had his own spin on the "mantenna."

"I don't know what it's called, but everybody has some kind of signal. Some of us just don't listen to it and use it. Remember when I was dating that girl from Downsview?"

"Yea."

"Well, I knew something was wrong straight off, but she was red hot, and I had to pursue. If someone has to give you a schedule to see them, that's a big clue that something is off. In the end, her boyfriend stuck a gun in my face. I'm lucky to still have these handsome features. Now a woman in my place would say, "Hey, something seems wrong here," and then she would walk away if she trusted herself. But we men need to have our heads bashed in and the blood run down our faces before we heed the warnings."

"So we are idiots, then?"

"No, we are socialized to be macho, so we run head-on into a brick wall and think we are going to conquer it with all this testosterone that we have, although it is obviously senseless. We are like matadors. We know the bull is going to gore us, but we rush forward with our red flag."

"I guess that's why women's intuition is so popular. It's because they use it."

"That's what I think. The only intuition we use is testosterone. It makes us chase skirts and start useless fights in bars."

"Stereotypical, and it proves my point that we are stupid."

"Well, I didn't say we were; I said we act like it. The thing is, even with women, it's a matter of trusting yourself because if you can sense danger but don't act to protect yourself, it's still useless."

I thought that my father and Paul could both be right. What I really wanted was to have the ability to perceive myself and where I wanted to be. I also wanted the presence of mind to use that ability. If ever I wanted that sixth sense, I needed it now.

10 May 2006

I want to listen to my gut feelings and stop procrastinating about my life. Lethargy of the mind translates to the same lack of vitality in the body. Mostly I want to be responsible for my own life and the decisions that I make. I don't want to blame anyone for my failures. Who else could have kept my marriage together but me? Who else allowed my wife to leave; who else should have completed a master's degree? If I subconsciously or consciously assimilated a skewed view of the world, wasn't that also my fault? If my faith in my ability to do my job is shaken, isn't it my own responsibility to restore it? After saying all this, don't I have the phallic thrust to redeem myself? What in God's name is phallic thrust? It's that male thing again, where everything must be a hard push.

Simmering under everything is my need to call Debbie up and say I'm sorry about the way we left things. I don't know what she thinks about why we fell apart. Why would she know what to think, when there was no explanation on my part? But how do you tell someone you're sorry for wasting two years of her life, and is it something she wants to hear? Do I stir up old wounds? But I want her to know that I take full responsibility for what happened. (When did that happen?) There is a corner of my mind where I entertain the thought of getting her back. What a joke, like she would allow me to waste more of her time. And if I can't find the courage to say sorry, how am I going to say I want you back? "Stand up like a man and take what you want." That's what my mother would tell me. Although I am a man, I know I can't always just take. I will have to ask, even coax my way into the place that I want to be.

Taking responsibility is not always the easiest thing to do. The brutal reality is that I had what I wanted, and I let it go. Debbie said many times, "John, do you want this to work?" And all I could muster was a general, "What do you think?"—a question to answer a question because I didn't have a strong reply.

"If I knew what to think, I wouldn't ask."

"I'm here, aren't I?"

"So you think presenting your body is enough? Your mind isn't here. You are generally disinterested in anything including me ... sex... Maybe you still do your job because you have to. I try to talk to you, and you respond with monosyllables and meaningless phrases."

"So I have to utter a thousand words to be meaningful? It's like conversation has to be a full length article with you."

"No, you just have to participate like you mean it."

"Seriously, I don't know what you want from me."

"Do you want a list? How about getting to know who you are?"

"See, this is why I'm not participating. I don't even know what that question means. Is there a manual on me that you want? We're married. You know where I work, what I do, what I eat, where I live, and where I sleep, so I don't understand how don't know who I am. I know who you are, and I don't have a manual on you."

"Do you really know who I am? You don't know what I want—like more openness, less secrecy, more intimacy, more of you. Your cynicism about manuals doesn't help."

"These conversations are really tedious. We have them every two days, and I don't understand what they mean, and we make no progress."

"Well, maybe life without me will be a little less tiresome."

Those were her famous last words. Here I am in life without her, and it is even more tedious and less interesting. And from this distance, I know what she meant about knowing someone. Perhaps I always knew. I think of myself as the soccer club that sold a promising player to another club; now the player is back on the market, but the price is so over the top that the original club cannot afford to buy him back. What's the lesson here? Never be too quick to part with what you have, especially when you know its value. Sometimes holding on can be hard, but the returns will be good. I want to collect on the windfall.

13 May 2006

Increasingly, I am having lunch with Maya alone. Paul is busy with whatever they do over there at the Ministry of Finance. He has lunch at his desk, but we are still all in debt. I read it in the *Chronicle*, and I saw it on Toronto TV: Everywhere there is debt and budget cuts. Even Paul said that if he were going to have a big belly from his lack of mobility, the Province should have a big bank account to take care of the transit, roads, housing, and other major necessities that allow a city to be world-class. We can't always get what we want, I suppose. Maya is great company anyway. She is the best, and apart from Debbie, she is the most fascinating woman. I never know what she is going to say next. The fact that she is my cousin makes me think about bloodlines and how I had missed the boat.

"So, Kingston—are you still going?"

We were at the Keg on York. I was having the New York steak, and Maya was having the seafood wrap.

"Sure, maybe this weekend."

"Wow, this weekend. When did you decide?"

"Just now, when you asked, and now that I have committed to it, I guess I'll have to go. I don't know what it will accomplish."

"The sooner you go, the sooner you'll find out. I don't think it will solve your problems, but it might give you perspective."

"I guess I need all the perspective I can get. Why is it that something that happened so long ago can still have such an impact?"

"You've asked that question many times, and I ask again, don't you have a degree in psychology? Listen, you have a problem with your mother sleeping with various men because there is no way you can be objective about it. We never see things as they are; we see them as *we* are. I know it's your mother and you have her on a pedestal, so perhaps your reaction is natural. Nobody wants to think of his mother as some kind of suburban floozy. Yet it's entirely possible that somebody else in your circumstances might not be affected the same way. How would this other person see it? Perhaps he or she would say, 'Okay, my mother sleeps around; she displays nontraditional behaviour, but that's her way. It's not my way, and I am not going to penalize her for it.' My father is an alcoholic, and I'm told there's a good chance that I could become one too. What do I do? I drink as moderately as possible. My father's way is not mine. Do I hate my father for giving me his genes? No, I do not. I have control over what I do with myself."

I remembered there were no bottles of alcohol in Aunt Daphne's house. If you have a problem, one way of eliminating the danger of regression is to cut out the temptation.

"But we are talking about two different things here. I am not so sure about your analogy. My mother runs an upper-middle-class sex shop, and your father can't help drinking. One's an addiction; the other is by choice."

"Is it? Who's to say your mother isn't battling an addiction? Have you ever looked at it that way? I think not."

"Addictions are caused by emotional problems left unattended. It's difficult to see what emotional problems my mother could have."

I looked at my fork and thought of the many prongs of addiction, but I couldn't see how my mother would be associated with any of these prongs.

"You are primed for an addiction, then. But we never know, do we? Sometimes the people we are closest to are the ones we know the least. We all have addictions; it's just that some seem worse than others—but they are all the same things. It's our social conditioning that leads us to believe that one is worse than the other."

"So I should treat her lifestyle like any other addiction?"

"I'm not telling you how to treat anything. How can you treat something you don't even understand? And if you don't understand, you can never empathise. I don't want to play down your feelings. You are the one feeling it, but Aunt Martha has her own feelings. Nothing has changed in the way I feel about her. She is still my cool aunt."

"But you are different."

"How so? If it were your father who was traipsing about with various women, would you feel the same way?"

"I don't know."

"The fact that you don't know answers my question. It's one system or grade for him, and another set for her."

"You know what I don't want to talk about gender divide. I maintain that how you feel is different. You never lived with her, and she isn't your mother. She didn't hold you to her bosom."

I touched my chest just about where my nipples were, and Maya laughed.

"You're right, you are the one who got suckled." She stuck her tongue out to mock me.

"So you think my mother is addicted to sex?"

"I don't know. I am looking at an unexplored perspective. Sex can be addictive as anything else."

"I wish she was addicted to something else—like food."

"She'd be overweight."

"To sweets."

"She'd lose her teeth."

"Even to marijuana. You've incorporated it into your lifestyle, and it's not bothering you."

"Everything is not for everyone. You've just named two things that involve eating, so I assume you'd rather her eating than having sex. And the third thing you named would make her eat a lot too. You need to let this go. Scabs on sores get no better if you keep picking at them. You are holding on so tightly to this one thing that I don't think there's any room left for you to accept anything else. Isn't it tiring to do that? Variety is the spice of life, and we can hold onto many different things if we choose to. You know we can make ourselves blind to the things we are doing because we are so consumed by our own convictions and morality. Let it go, not for her sake but for yours. Do you think if you just release all of this negative stuff, you'd be letting her off the hook?"

"Probably."

I cut into my steak and brought the fork to my mouth, looking at the four prongs again. Even this inanimate object needed more than one point to function well.

"You're the holder of the fort; you're letting her know that what she is doing is wrong. But tell me this—who's the holder of your fort? I am telling you as a friend and as family that you need to drop this matter like it were bad news from yesterday. Throw it out like you do the paper after you read it … oh, bad example—I forget that you hold onto those. But you know what I mean. Focus on John."

"I know that's what I need to do. It's just that when you've been holding onto one thing for a very long time, it's hard to let go. It's like, what will I hold onto now? But you know what? I am starting to, slowly but surely. I'm at the point where I just don't want to think about it; I want to take practical steps. I've picked up application forms to do my master's degree."

"Great. Debbie tried for almost two years to get you to do this, and you've finally taken a step. She should hear this."

"It's ironic, isn't it? I introduced you to her, and you became friends. My marriage failed, and you're still friends."

"That's life; I'm sorry. Just because you pissed on your marriage doesn't mean I should drop a good friend. Besides, I can be a good friend to both of you."

"Do you two talk about me?"

"Oh, John, I'll discuss almost anything with you, but you are stepping on uncharted territory."

Okay, forget it. It was stupid of me to ask, anyway."

In my mind's eye, I could see them having a conversation about me. I just couldn't pinpoint the specifics. I wasn't even sure if I wanted to.

"John, I would never say anything bad about you—I think you know that—and as undeserving as you may be of her protection, neither would she."

"I had that coming. While we are on the subject of my wife, and it's the first time I'll say this out loud and it's because I trust you, I trust you a lot, and please do not think me silly or egotistical or a narcissist because I am not—but do you think my wife would take me back? What are the chances?"

It was hell to get that out. I felt weak all over to the point where I paused before picking up the knife and fork lest they fell out of my hands and embarrassed me.

"Honestly, I don't know."

She was trying intently to hold the wrap as carefully as possible so it wouldn't unravel. It would be a little more challenging to eat droppings of crab meat, shrimp, and all the other stuff if this happened.

"You never really know someone else's thoughts, and it doesn't matter how much that person says. My suggestion to you is the same as usual—talk to her. Stop reading her columns in the newspaper; you aren't telepathic, and neither is she. In any case, I don't know if telepathy would be right for you, given the fact that a part of why your marriage failed was your lack of speech or your lack of openness. Call her on the phone, go talk to her in person, or, if you are extremely shy, send her a personal note. I would rather you not be shy. Be bold. That's what the situation calls for, and things tend to fall into place when you go for it."

"That's easy for you to say because that's what you are."

"Not from the outset. But in sales and marketing, you give a lot of presentations, and you'd better be daring. The field I chose sort of made me who I am. Nobody buys pretty pictures from the timid. If you're timid, you aren't sure, and if you're unsure, how will you sell?"

"Couldn't it be that it's because of who you that you chose that field?"

"That's a good question, and maybe you should answer it yourself."

And that's what it boils down to: I have to be bold. I've already made the decision to contact Debbie, although the when or how isn't decided yet. I've also considered whether I'm ready to make that contact. If I go to her the same way I was before, would there be any difference? But if I wait until I think I'm ready, would I ever make the move? Better an imperfect move than perfect inertia.

16 May 2006

I never thought out my decision about when to go to Kingston, yet on the weekend I got up and went about putting things in place to go. I put my favourite Bob Marley, Jimmy Cliff, and Luciano CDs in the jeep; my father had introduced me to these musicians, and he could tell anybody what they needed to know about music, especially the Jamaican stuff. I had also been to my father's birthplace, where music is the food and the entire meaning of life. I had gone once before to Jamaica to see my paternal grandparents, and I've been told my maternal grandparents were both from St. Elizabeth, but I've never been there. It's still on the agenda because it would be nice to see my mother's roots.

I also put the Fugees and Bedouin Soundclash in there to mix things up a bit. I had filled up on gas the night before; I threw the various parts of the broken, dismantled chair in the back, not knowing what I would do with them but knowing I would think of something. I packed a bag of overnight clothes, not knowing how long I would stay, and then I took off, leaving Toronto behind. *Why didn't I do this before?* I asked myself as I left all that I was in touch with and retuned with the limestone city.

Even when I was a boy, the rugged, unspoilt beauty of Kingston had taken my breath away. The blue-green ocean, the waves rolling in, the surrounding greenness, and the simple unhurried vibe were a feast for the senses. I am not going to compare it to St. Ann, Jamaica, but being in Kingston, Ontario, is almost like being in another country—the initial beauty bowls you over. It has the most beautiful waterfront in the world. Passing people sailed and some enjoyed a round of golf. I kept thinking, *What will I accomplish? What will I accomplish?* And at the same time, I heard Maya's parting comment to me, "*Try not to be too analytical with anything that happens; just let it come. Remember, you're not at your desk.*" That sounded like good advice, but what was the "it" that might come? If one was looking for something, shouldn't one know what one was looking for? And how would I know if I had found it? I got into Lansdowne, parked at my father's house, and went inside using the key that my father had given me. My father and Joy were away; he was touring Japan with the music my mother said would not make it, while I searched Kingston, Ontario for a little part of myself.

I changed into something fit for a walk and decided the first order of business would be to get rid of the broken chair—the unnecessary burden. Instantly, and for no apparent reason, I knew I'd do it by the river. I took the various parts and placed them in one of the large garbage bags my father kept under the sink, throwing in a box of matches and some old newspaper. Then I took the walk that I had always loved. There weren't any people around; the air was still a bit nippy, even though it was warm for the time of the year. I went to the river, and there I set up a semi-pyramid made of legs, arms, back, and the rest of the body of a chair, with a foundation of newspaper. I would burn it at the proverbial stake.

I thought about saying a prayer of good-bye—a chant perhaps, or any parting ritual. Death has always had its rites and procedures, and there is usually a special significance associated with the destiny of the deceased. However, I couldn't think of anything but a burning itch to start the fire. The only rites of passage for the chair would be the fire itself, the great purifier. Should I have felt something? With the matchstick twirling between my thumb and forefinger, all I felt was the anxiety to get on with it. The stick struck the box with such great force it didn't light. The next attempt, more gentle, was successful. The fire started with a lot of smoke at first, and as I watched it shooting up in short and tall red orange fingers, I looked around and saw the place where I had gone swimming, where we had barbequed all kinds of meats, where I had hung out with neighbourhood boys, and where I had sat and talked to my father. There were many good memories, and now it would be the place where I burned to ashes a part of my life I didn't want.

After the event—it was an event—I looked at the ashes, even examined them and saw how one seemingly monumental image/action that had affected my life could be reduced to dust, dust that flew here and there with the breeze, mingled with the earth, and went to its own extinction. I didn't want to see the remaining ashes, and I certainly didn't want to see the black spot, so I covered it up with dirt from another spot. It wasn't a cover up; in time, the spot would have gone away naturally. I just wanted to see fresh, new dirt. It was a good image to walk away with—newness. Now I need to adjust my mind to this death. By burning the evidence, can I burn the crime?

After that, I sat on one of my large stones, throwing rocks into the river and watching them disappear the instant they hit the surface of the water. Plunk, plunk. There was no struggle; sinking was the natural order of things. What I thought about as I did this was the absurdity of holding onto things, especially the ones I had no control over. Was it all that simple? I had left Toronto at 7:00 AM, gotten to Lansdowne minutes to 10:00, and had incinerated a piece of my past and hopefully a piece of my psyche by 11:00 AM. It felt like I had done a lot. I didn't know if the burning of the chair would translate into any purification for me, but it was a good beginning.

I thought I would do something relaxing, like going down to the waterfront, eating some Caribbean food at Cynthia's, or staying the night and going to the Roof Club, but after the burning, I felt like I had to be on the move. It was an event that needed another event. It wasn't an anxious need but a calm, decisive prodding to take the next step. The overnight bag wasn't necessary because I decided to head back to Toronto. My only problem then was choosing which Bob to play. I started with "Burnin' and Lootin'" and loved the lines, "Burnin' all pollution / Burnin' all illusion." I guessed I loved the Bob of fire.

When I got home, I took down the picture of Debbie. Even without the photograph, she was still there, present in a thousand different memories, and I could still talk to her without the frame. I was not going to hang the photograph again until I had spoken to Debbie. I had constructed an enclosure around her picture and around myself. It was time to work outside the borders. I kept bottles of Absolut Vodka, Canadian Club, and Johnnie Walker, along with beer in the house; it had been a source of contention with Debbie. I had spruced up the house recently, and now I thought I would further clean house by hosing down the sink with the contents of the bottles. The beers could stay, though, because Debbie had one every now and again. Maya told me once that Aunt Daphne hadn't allowed Uncle Mike to drink outside the house; maybe this would become my policy too, so I could monitor myself. This would be one of the borders I could work within. Even though I wanted to work outside most of my borders, some of the boundaries could stay—they would be good for my protection and security.

18 May 2006

On Sundays, I usually relax by taking in an art exhibition, watching movies, reading the papers, and so on, but this Sunday, I felt a huge burst of testosterone, like I could go into a boxing ring with a heavyweight champion and win. I joined Paul at the mini-stadium on the other side of town for a game of football.

"It's been a while since you played, man. Sure you're up for this?"

"Yes. I'm catching up; I guess it's time."

"These guys are tough, so gear up; this is no Forest Hill, pretty-boy match. This will probably be a scrappy dog fight with a lot of rough tackles."

"I'm ready, I'm ready."

And that was exactly how I felt. Usually I liked to play forward because that was where the glory lay, but on this day I decided to go into the trenches. I played defence, and I did it strongly and aggressively, cutting off all spaces and squeezing the attack in tight, difficult positions. I felt like a superhero, denying shots, denying penetration, closing the distance between myself and whoever had the ball. My choice of angles allowed me to block any attempted shots. I won possession; I attacked and tackled as if my life were depending on it. The sweat, the drive, and the will to win just pushed me on.

"Man, you played like a beast out there. What's gotten into you? You are usually decent in defence, but today, hats off to you. You were great."

"I felt pumped, I'll admit."

"What the hell did you drink in Kingston? Did they make a new energy drink from fresh water?"

"No energy drink, just new energy, perhaps."

"Whatever it is, keep using it; it's working for you, at least on the football pitch. I wish I could dig deeper to get to the source of your energy, but I have to run. I'm attending afternoon mass."

"So you are Catholic now? Don't answer; you met a Catholic, church-going girl. So, mass is a social event now?"

"Aren't all churches, whether they hold mass, prayer meetings, or rallies? If you want to meet women, you have to go where they are, and many of them are at church."

"I admire your efforts. I'll give you an *A*."

"Got to meet them halfway and show some interests in their activities."

"After that, then what?"

"Who knows? We'll see where it leads. It's all the same thing, trial and error, but ultimately—despite what we say and do—we all want the same thing. The same thing that you tried to have: one great girl to love and make a family with."

I never expected to hear those words from Paul's mouth, but who did I really know, except for myself? Who knows anybody else for sure? We're surrounded by people we speak to every day. We see the things they do, and we may know some of their opinions, but are these enough to judge them on, to say we know them? It's safer to say I know someone to an extent than to say I know someone full stop. There are too many layers to an individual.

After the adrenaline of football, I geared down a bit. I left my home for the artsy home of Maya. Her deliberate, minimalist approach to furniture often leaves me with the feeling I am in a house that is only partly furnished, but as she often tells me, she only needs the essentials. All the unnecessary furnishings would only get in the way, constituting baggage and collecting dust, and reminding me of my own home. She was at the tail end of watching the movie *Crash*.

"Is that the movie about racism?"

"Yes, but there's more to it than that."

"Like what?"

"Well, I think the movie is good at showing us how we judge everybody else's behaviour, but we don't judge ourselves, when in fact we are all capable of unpleasant, hostile, and threatening behaviour."

"That sounds pretty deep. Good thing I came at the end."

"You are trying to be funny. Remember when I used to follow you around?"

"How could I forget? You were like a puppy, or Mary's little lamb. Aunt Daphne used to tell you not to follow me so much. You asked her why, and she told you that I was older, that I was a boy and did boy things, and that boys needed their space. But of course, you didn't listen and continued to follow me."

"Did you mind?"

"Never."

"I don't believe that because you used to tell me to bug off." Maya got up and went into the kitchen. I heard the door of the fridge open and close.

"Oh, that was just for show. When I was a boy, it was flattering to think I was being trailed because I was so darn interesting, and when I got older, the company of a pretty girl was an asset. I used to get all sorts of favours from guys who just wanted my cousin's number. Now you are my advisor, and now I follow you around. Do you mind?"

"First, you don't follow me around, and second, you have been an asset too. Do you know how many girls have asked me about the handsome guy who keeps himself to himself?"

"You should have told them John De Baptist, crying in the wilderness, knowing that he will lose his head to have it presented to someone on a silver platter." I heard the hiss of the stopper on a beer.

"Speaking of wilderness, I did not expect you back from Kingston until this evening. What happened?"

"Do you think Kingston is a wilderness?"

She laughed out loud, came back to the living room, and handed me a Laker Strong.

"No. It's just somewhere out there, and it has a lot of prisons, which kind of make me think about remoteness. You know, like Alcatraz Island and that infamous federal penitentiary. It's just how the mind works, that's all."

"Well, there's a lot more to it than that. I thought I might have stayed overnight too; I even carried a bag with clothes, but I came back early. I went, I burned that God forsaken chair, and here I am."

"So you went to your father's house just to burn a chair?"

"No, I burned the chair by Shrewsbury River."

"Interesting."

"How so?"

"You got rid of an unsavoury part of your history in one of your favourite places. Was it a cleansing of sort?"

"You mean with the water?"

"No, I meant all the good things you did and enjoyed at that river would drown out the memories of the chair somehow?"

"I don't know. I didn't think about it."

"Did you think about the duality taking place there?"

"What duality?"

"The fire you made by your favourite water spot. The warmth, the coolness, the wet and the dry. I don't know. There seems to be something going on there, but damn if I know what it is."

I drank the beer, enjoying the coldness of it. There is no duality in a Laker Strong; it is just beer, simple, strong, and cheap.

"It's always this marketing thing with you. It makes you see more in images than there really is, and that's what you sell—codes and connections to people's minds. As I said, I had no premeditated ideas. I did think about fire being a purifier as I watched the chair go up in flames and disintegrate to ashes, but that's about it for the metaphor. Yet, water could be a purifier too, right?"

"Yes, they are opposite and the same, which is weird. Tell me this though: How are you going to explain the absence of the chair to your mother if she enquires?"

"I'll tell her I burned it."

"So you are ready for an all-out confrontation?" She slipped the DVD out of the entertainment system and looked around for the case.

"Why not? I want to tell her how I feel about what she did, what she is probably still doing. Do you know, if I want to go over the house, I call first; I don't want an unexpected encounter. Anyway, I want to do it straight out, without all the figurative skirting that usually takes place."

"Telling her you burned her heirloom will certainly help." She found the case and slipped the DVD in it.

"It's not hers anymore; she gave it to me, and I did what I wanted with it. In any case, you can never gauge her reaction to anything. I am not sure if that damn chair meant anything at all to her in the first place." The beer was just what I needed after chasing ball for much of the afternoon.

"Question: Are you going to confront your mother first, or will you approach your ex-wife first?" She hit the source button and changed the television from DVD to TV. A documentary on migrating birds was on.

"Is it important which one happens first? Now you've given me something else to think about. It's not as if I have a schedule for any of these things."

"I'm not saying any of them takes priority; I'm just curious. You are about to face two very important women in your life, perhaps the two most important, one you are going to try to win back and the other one I'm sure you're going to fight with. You are in a battle either way. I just wanted to know which one you're going to start with first."

The birds flew in groups and relied on each other for survival.

"You've just made this a little bit more complex in my head, but I'm going to do this like a to-do list, with my priority at the top."

"What's your priority, John?"

"Debbie. I've spent too much time on my mother already."

The birds exploited the winds so they could go for long distances without using too much effort. That was what my father had been talking about—refining an art and being smart to use less muscle. We could learn from those birds.

"Yes, and that is the reason that you are bound so tightly to her."

19 May 2006

I've made the decision to work on my master's degree part-time. It isn't necessary to give up my job. I am moving up the ranks based on my experience, and I will take this degree for self-development and a better understanding of the profession I have chosen. It might assist me in a promotion, but I'm not concerned about that. I'm more concerned about giving my best to the people I see every day, and perhaps I want to live up to my wife's expectations and be on par with her. I haven't grown accustomed to saying ex-wife, ex being a prefix of the past.

I completed the form and got ready to do what I should have done when I completed my first degree. I would drop the form on campus before the deadline. Why has it been so hard for me to do this up to now? Why has it taken years? It's not like I can't afford it. My father's music and my mother's twisted art bought me a good education. I can't say my mother didn't look after me in that regard. I could have even done a PhD if I were just a little more ardent. Well, completing a form was the easy part. I decided to write my wife a letter, and that would be the hard part. I thought about calling, but I decided on writing. She could have my thoughts and feelings in black and white—a hard copy that could not be erased. Where did I begin to find the words? I thought about saying I'd been stupid or a fool, but that would not do because if I were a fool, I'd probably still be one, and why would she even consider taking back an idiot? What message did I want to convey?

In the end, this was what I wrote:

May 2006
Dear Debbie,

I am very sorry. This apology is long overdue, so maybe it's not even valid (past due). I have to try anyway because I have to take responsibility for our failed marriage. I must let you know that I have thought long and hard about all this, and even though it may not seem that way to you, I have not taken my responsibility lightly. I have my reasons for not opening up to you, but I will not use that as an excuse, as I am the only one responsible for my actions or lack thereof.

I am especially sorry about the not-opening-up part because maybe if I had, we could have worked things out. Without rambling on, I would like to speak to you face-to-face to explain things a bit more. If you agree, you can choose the time and place. If I don't hear from you, I'll take it that you are not interested in talking or meeting.

John

I read it over a thousand times. Was it going to impress her? I wasn't trying to impress; I was trying to persuade. Was it persuasive? I wasn't sure. This wasn't something I could seek an opinion on, not even from Maya. I had to write my own words to my own wife with no outside editorial input. If I failed at this, it would be my own words failing me. What do women want? They want you to say you're sorry when you do wrong to them.

My letter said sorry. They want you to take responsibility for your actions, to be a man about it, and I took responsibility. They want you to open up and be intimate; the letter implied that I would. They want to have an input into things and have some control; I had left the next step up to her. Hell, a lot of the things I think women want are some of the same things that I want. It is all a choice of words, I suppose. I'm sure I wouldn't use the word *intimacy* normally, but I want closeness. What's the difference? Intuition, gut feeling.

Now the letter is written, and it's time to deliver it. I know that once it leaves my hands, that's it; there's no going back. I toyed with the idea of making changes, wondering if it were perfect, but I know it isn't the flawlessness of the note that has me loitering; it's the unknown response. The unknown world—I will have to trod into it and explore.

21 May 2006

Since sending the letter, it's all I can think about. I'd always thought that to be a man I had to be in control of whatever situation I was in. Well, isn't that laughable, since I'm waiting on another person's decision to take my next step. I'm totally powerless. I can either laugh or cry. But crying isn't allowed—not in my world. That's the reason I end up drinking in bars, picking stupid fights, and nursing a busted lip on some weekends. (Then, during the weekday, I counsel others on substance abuse.) That's one of the reasons Maya is with us a lot because Paul's presence is also a testosterone-fuelled one, and that doesn't help. When she's with us, we go to cafés, and she brings a certain equilibrium to the toughness. If water isn't allowed to run from the eyes, then something else has to flow, and that ends up being blood from the busted lip or alcohol from a bottle. It sounds stupid, and it also looks as stupid on paper, stupidness in black and white.

What do you do when you want to take your mind off anything? You take action with whatever will occupy the mind. That's what I do. I repainted the interior of the condo, even though it was totally unnecessary. Between the exerted energy and the paint fumes, I held at bay the heady feeling of expectations. I also frittered the time away deciding between beige, off white, or light yellow, while skipping over names like canary and fuchsia. To look at paint charts, it seems you have to be an artist, looking at a palette. Well, the point is to use time, so fine—I can pretend. I've saved my bedroom for last because I will need refuge from the fumes. There are old newspapers everywhere I look, reminding me of things past and making me think how quickly the apartment would burn if it caught fire. Really, that is just morbid.

Along with the paints, I bought some tiles from the hardware store. We had been talking about retiling the bathroom walls but hadn't got around to it. Now I have tiles stacked on the floor along with the old newspapers. The stale news was mostly *Chronicle* refuse that I've poured over trying to get a feel for my wife. In the middle of all this repainting, I learnt that a day after I delivered the letter, Debbie went to St. Lucia to cover their jazz festival. I chose white paint after much consideration. It is easier to get dirty but brilliantly and blindingly white at first. It makes me think of purity.

Since she was away, there were more days of waiting. These things usually go on for a week. Nothing to do but continue to paint, dig up old tiles, and put down new ones. At the rate at which I'm going, I could tear the entire condo down and build it back up. I started on the tiles, making the bathroom a construction area. Who was I kidding? I was going to need help on this, so I convinced Paul to assist me a couple of evenings, and if necessary, on the weekend. Laying tiles and grouting was not my forte.

"It's not going to be easy, man. I move figures for a living, not tiles. The hardest part is going to be removing the old stuff and getting the surface clean and prepared for the new ones."

I knew what he meant. Removing the old is always challenging, especially old actions and old thoughts.

"Well, let's get the hard part out of the way, then."

"What's your hurry, and why are you doing this? There's nothing wrong with these tiles. Are you selling?"

"Only to myself. I want to bring a newness to the place."

"You've succeeded. I almost feel virginal, baptismal almost, in this white-painted house."

"Glad you approve. Maybe I should do more."

"Let's stick to the task at hand."

So we got to digging and chipping off the old tiles, revealing a mask of substrate substance beneath.

"Good thing I am committed to this; it's challenging."

"I told you it was hard work, man; that's why they pay professionals to do this. Why are you doing this again?"

"Under normal circumstances, I would call in a pro, but I just wanted to get my hands dirty. I just wanted to know that I had a hand in creating something from scratch and having the satisfaction of having it turn out good, especially something I don't usually do. Ever had that feeling?"

"Sure."

We got through the retiling and the grout work between bottles of Red Stripe and take-out orders from Island Grill. Paul even shared my sense of accomplishment in what we achieved. I threw out the old papers, empty paint tins, and paint-soaked rags; I cleaned brushes, trowels, and pails. I basked in the newfound space of my home and hoped for as clean a start as my white walls and new tiles.

25 May 2006

My mother never officially invited me to any of her exhibitions. She knew how I felt about her nontraditional, controversial, experimental artwork. I wanted to have an open mind about it, but the nonconformist nature of it always overpowered the openness I sought. So when she called inviting me to the opening of The Rebelvisionaries, I was taken off guard, and I said yes even before I thought about it. She had invited Maya too. I was sure my mother didn't have to sell it to Maya; she just had to tell her when. The exhibitions were social events, with finger foods eaten while the cutting-edge pieces were discussed. The guest speaker was the chairwoman of the Art Institute of Toronto, who excited us about new trends in art and how alive the pieces were. It was the usual discourse of the art establishment, one the unschooled knows nothing about.

For the rest of the evening, that was all I heard, the new, revolutionary art capturing the imagination with its contemporary feel. It was both risqué and engaging.

"It certainly gets your attention," Maya said.

"Yea, it does, but more like a car accident you can't get out of your head—crushed and bent metal."

"That's your problem right there; you've got to learn to look beyond the obvious to the art, to the unique. Open up a bit."

"I can't get beyond knowing that I am looking at metal, rods, rivets, and all that. I don't necessarily find all of this aesthetically pleasing."

"That much is clear. I don't know if art is always meant to be beautiful. If it's a slice of life ,as we say, how can it always be beautiful when life is not?"

"I like it beautiful, though."

"Perhaps we all do. But what about something designed to make us think differently about society or about how we live or think? I don't know, but maybe this kind of art is supposed to teach us we shouldn't give importance to predictability. Instead, we should give in to new kinds of creativity. Perhaps we need to find the beauty in that."

We walked from piece to piece, standing before each, looking for something. I was searching for meaning, something to walk away with.

"It's hard to turn your head around. You go into a gallery; you see paintings, sculptures, et cetera. That's what I'm used to."

"You are such a traditionalist, almost reactionary. See beyond the paint and canvas art. Look to the present form and its new function. You know, tradition is only made by time and nothing else. Tradition doesn't necessarily make something good or valid."

"Of course it does. Things that are long established gain validity in the mind."

"In some parts of the world, female circumcision is a tradition. In my mind, this tradition isn't good."

"I suppose not."

Maya made good sense about tradition, whether it pertained to art or anything else. It was all the same. We could start new traditions.

"You are so dismissive of things that are not as you see them or how you want them to be. Bend a little."

We passed more bent metal, and I wondered if I were more flexible and could bend into all sorts of angles like the piece I was looking at, whether I would be any freer.

"Oh sure, I can be pliable."

"It's probably in your best interests. Those pieces make for great conversations."

"I'm sure they do."

"Have you seen the piece that Mom has?"

"I didn't even know she would be interested, much less to own a piece."

"Well, there you go. My mother may be old, but she is not cold. It's a sailing ship that's made from something that looks like aluminium."

"I admire her tolerance."

"You don't even like one piece?"

"Oh, I don't know, I suppose that fender-bender guy playing the guitar and that projecting steel playing drums are not too bad."

"Well, there you go. Your appreciation up by two."

"I don't know if it's appreciation or absorption. I am surrounded by it so much, I'm starting to see some I like."

"You take a long time to absorb. It's not as if you weren't surrounded by this stuff from a young age."

"Yes, I was practically tripping over the stuff. Some of them were like missiles or projectiles. It's a wonder I wasn't gored. I associate it with my mother, so I kept it away from me. I don't even know why she invited me here."

Everything had an edge in this place.

"Maybe because she's your mother and wants to get close to you?"

"She hasn't done this before. The only thing she's ever wanted to do was bust my balls, verbal castration."

"I'm sure she meant well. She had a Jamaican mother, and you know they always want to toughen boys up. The entire society does that, even here in Canada. It's sort of a universal culture. Boys must be tough."

"Yea, well, maybe we need to change the culture because as a boy growing up, I sure could have used some soft love."

Now there was a tradition I thought we could readily change. I guessed Maya had proved her point even without knowing it.

"Is that a new therapy term? Tough love, soft love."

"No, I just made that up, but it seems logical because that's what I needed. She would always say things like, "Get over it; you're a man," as if by virtue of being male, I had a solution to all my problems. She got a thrill by literally holding me by the balls and squeezing to see if they were still there. If you walked into the room and didn't know what she was doing, you would think some Oedipus thing was going on."

"Our mothers—and this is especially true for black mothers—don't care if we're ten or twenty; they own us because they carried us into this world. She basically owned your balls and that other thing that's down there too."

"I am so happy that you find my emasculation amusing. Did Aunt Daphne ever grab onto any of your parts?"

"Maybe you shouldn't equate your manhood to your penis and balls so much. The only difference between you and me, dear fellow, is that I don't have hanging, dangling parts that are easily clutched."

"Very funny. I'm not even talking so much about her holding and squeezing as about the things she said. Shit, they were both bad. She gave me the impression she was as hard as all this steel that surrounds us right now."

"Maybe it was an impression."

"Well, she succeeded in making one hell of an impression."

I barely spoke to my mother all evening. She was busy being curator and host to art lovers. Moving from group to group, she touched, almost caressed some of the pieces with those hands, gesticulating and telling people about the artist and the value of the pieces. I never knew how they estimated art prices in general, and it was worse with this contemporary stuff. I have heard prices quoted for paintings that I would never make by working in this lifetime. How do you put a value on paints, canvas, skill, imagination, and reputation? I had no answer.

I wondered if it was at events like these that she met the men—art lovers, art buyers, probably the steel-buying kind. Did she catalogue them like she did the art collections? Did she have a database where she stored the art lovers and then called them up to ask whether they wanted to see more than her gallery? Did she collect them like pieces of artwork, and why would she do that? God, she was as beautiful as a swan, gliding to and fro, tall and elegant, inclining that long neck of hers to listen to the art crowd. I loved my mother, but I didn't love her lifestyle, but Jesus, couldn't I still accept her in spite of it? I could decide to do whatever I wanted to do.

We circled an installation called *Religion*. It was made with pieces of sticks put together to resemble a building, possibly a church.

"John, tell me you don't see that."

"See what? It's a very boxed-up church."

"That's what I see, too—religion in a box. Maybe it's religion as a box."

I really thought I could see it. There was very little space inside the contrivance. The concept and the lack of space made me feel a little breathless.

"This reminds me of your obsession with the incident of the Bible and marijuana."

"How so?"

"The way everything, including religion, is boxed up into parts without room for anything else to come in. Marijuana is associated with one religion, Rastafarianism, and the Bible with Christianity. To associate the two—marijuana and the Bible, I mean—is probably a sin. Yet, I see them coming from one source. There are just too many partitions."

"But that's life, isn't it?"

"Yea, but it's a life we've created."

"It's a coping mechanism."

I continued looking at the church. There were no steps, no grass, absolutely no adornment, just a boarded cubicle with defined, cramped legroom. The wooden slats that made it up had little gaps between them so you could see inside, no matter where you stood.

"I think we would cope better if we allowed ourselves to roam freely through the dividing walls. I know I sound like an idealist because I don't think it has to be the way it is. I don't see why we can't allow other things to come in."

We moved from the piece, but I couldn't help wondering if the slits and gaps in the work were there to allow the other things that Maya was talking about to come in.

My mother's car was in the garage. She didn't say what had happened to it, but like any good son should, I drove her home.

"What's wrong with the car?"

"Oh, it got a little nick. It's nothing that a good body man can't fix." She fidgeted in her seat and took a box of cigarettes from her bag.

"How did it happen?"

"The usual way these things happen—accidentally. Somebody is careless, and I get the back of my bumper dented in."

"So that person is going to pay to fix your car, I hope."

"Yes, that's how it works, isn't it?"

"Are the damages over a thousand dollars?"

"Yes."

"So the police were called?"

"Yes."

"That must have been some accident. Why didn't you call me?"

"What exactly would you have done? I'm still here, and that's all that counts. So what did you think of the show?"

"It brought about a lot of discussion."

"My niece tells me that a good band would have complimented it."

"Something edgy, I suppose."

"I detect a note of something in your tone. What is it? Did your mother's postmodern art offend you?"

"I don't like it when you speak to me as if you were someone other than my mother."

"It's easier for me, especially when I am talking to you about a reevaluation of concepts. I asked you about the show, and all you can tell me is that there was a lot of discussion. I expect something specific about vision, progressiveness, or even a shift in something. What will I do with you?"

"I don't have your eye."

"I don't want you to. We all have our own sensory perception."

"Whatever that means."

She sighed deeply, perhaps to express sadness or fatigue at my unwillingness to be a disinterested critic or to at least have some sympathetic participation.

"Do you know a band that might be appropriate?"

"It's best to ask Maya. She is up with that kind of stuff. I am surprised she didn't give you a list already."

"We didn't talk long. I had to mingle with as many viewers as possible to get feedback on the show and to let them know I value their time and opinions. The piped music in the gallery always does the job, but a band is a good idea. The more I think about it, the more I like it. I am not just showing and selling art; I am involved with a culture, and that's a living, growing thing. A band is interactive. People will respond to it as part of what they're observing. Some people won't expect a band, so this would be a part of the exhibition where people bring their expectations and social norms into the gallery and either apply the norms or reverse them once they have seen the show. I'll speak to Maya."

Somewhere along talking about this musical posse, she had slipped a cigarette in her hand, and I could tell the craving was on.

"I am itching for a smoke. May I even dare ask?"

"No, it's not going to happen. We're in a closed car."

"We could open the windows."

Her left hand had the box of Virginia Slims, and her right had the single one. What else did her hands hold?

"No, that won't help. Let's try to preserve both our health."

"Do you know you're always trying to tell me what to do? You're my little conscience. I'll have to wait to do this at home. You would starve me of something I need."

"Need. Do you think smoking is a need? A need is shelter, clothing, food, and friends."

"So you are telling me about Maslow's hierarchy now?"

"Why did you invite me to this exhibition, anyway? You've never done so before."

"That's exactly why. I've never done it, and I wanted to do it. Now that's one thing I can take off my list of things to do. I invited John to an exhibition, and he came."

I should have asked her why she wanted to do it now, but I left it alone, and we drove the rest of the way in silence. For the entire trip, she held the single cigarette between her index and middle fingers. I knew she wanted to inhale or exhale.

She was barely out of the car before she started puffing. She handed me the keys to open the door. I followed behind the trail of smoke. It was the story of my life; I was either trailing behind her fumes or running from it.

"You really should quit."

"You want me to die, don't you?" She let her handbag fall on the settee, the hands of the bag touching one of her Norval Edwards pieces.

"On the contrary, I want you to live."

"Then how many times must I tell you? Quit and die; smoke and live."

"That's really a destructive way to look at it."

"No, not destructive—it's a survival mechanism. You do something for a long time, it becomes you. You stop, and it's almost like a mini-suicide."

"That's interpretive mumbo jumbo, and you know it. Is that the way you feel about the other things that have become a part of you?"

"What other things?"

The straps of her bag must have rattled the Norval Edwards because it came clattering off the side table, falling to the ground in a most profound way. It lost a couple of what I would call its limbs; they scattered on the floor like some weird assemblage.

I was never quite sure whether his work was intended to be installation or some other kind of art. It was installation now, modifying the way I saw it on the floor. The dissolution broke the line between art and life and gave me the feeling the veins in my head might explode. This was the point where I could either let everything drop or pursue the matter with some abandon. Like the concepts she wanted me to grasp, I was going to attack and confront the notions held by her and maybe by myself.

I threw caution to the wind. If I left my mother's house without saying what I wanted to say and getting the answers I wanted to get, then the chances were good it might never happen.

"I mean the men you've been sleeping with, the ones who have been traipsing in and out of this house since God knows when, disrespecting the other occupants of this house. Not you, of course. Do you have any respect for yourself or anybody else?" You call people crude if they are working class or if they do certain kinds of jobs, but how unsophisticated is your behaviour?"

She wasn't as angry as I expected her to be, or as she had always been before. She seemed more amused. Perhaps she believed this was just going to be another one of my tantrums, as she called them, and then it would dissolve into the nothingness that usually happened. Perhaps she was just getting old or tired.

"So you give me a ride home, and now you want to lecture me? You are like a man who takes a woman to dinner and wants sex at the end of the night."

"So some of them do take you to dinner."

"Do you realize that I am your mother? You answer to me, not the other way around. My private life has always been a concern of yours. Why don't you focus on your own?"

"All my life, you've been my mother, and that's the reason I give a damn. By the way, I am twenty-eight years old; I'm not ten anymore. If you own me because you are the woman who brought me here, by virtue of that same fact, I am laying claim to you too, so you answer to me also."

"Why do you care so much? It's not as if it affected you."

That made me angry.

"Why do I care? Let's see. How about because you are my mother, and right or wrong, men tend to put their mothers on a fucking pedestal. That's the reason we call black women empresses and queens—because we put them high up. And how would you know what affected me or how, when all you had time for was fucking men in fucking rocking chairs and God knows where else? When you found a little time for me it was only to tell me not to interrupt your sessions or to give me your version of how to be a man by searching for my scrotum. You fucking succeeded too. I lost my fucking balls, and I couldn't love my wife the way I wanted to. I had the perfect wife, and all I could see was you fucking man after man after man. I heard you telling me to be tough, like that was all it took to be manly. Look where all of this has gotten me! And you sit there, puffing on your long sticks of cancer, asking me why I care. Why the fuck don't you care more? If not for me, how about for your fucking self? You know how you talk about your fucking revolutions at your gallery? Talking about breaking traditional frames, structures, overthrowing categories that are artificially imposed, and all that intellectual art shit? Well, let's just have a fucking revolution here—right now. Can we do that, or is that just reserved for Queen Street?"

I was spent, so I sat down opposite her. She stubbed out the cigarette, and I noticed her hands were trembling.

"I had no idea."

"I don't know how you could sit there and say that, but now that you have an idea, tell me why you do it."

"It fills a void."

"A void? What void? You live in a nice home, you have a great job, and you even had not one but two great husbands."

"It gives me a kind of pleasure that none of those other things give me. I feel good about myself—powerful and in control—when I do it."

She folded her hands to steady them. I was seeing and hearing a side to my mother that I had never known was there. She was nervous. I had never seen her nervous before. I always thought she was in command.

"Jesus, you make it sound as if you lack self-esteem or something, and I don't believe that. If you do, couldn't you take pleasure and power from one source?"

"People lack things you don't see on the surface. It's complex. I take pleasure from the variety; one person cannot sustain it. I've tried to quit. It doesn't work. You were seven years old when we went to Vancouver for vacation. I saw somebody there who was supposed to know about these things. Here I am, the same."

"So it's safe to say we've got another ten to fifteen years of this?"

"Am I going to die at sixty-eight or seventy-three?"

"Oh, God." I sank deeper into the settee and closed my eyes against the thought.

"I am not saying I will not try to quit. I am just saying that I don't know how I will feel ten years from now. I don't know why I am telling you this, since it can only add fuel to your fire, but my car is in the garage because someone was angry with me and almost ran me off the road."

"It was one of them, wasn't it?" I opened my eyes to see her knowing that it could have been a different story.

"Yes."

I should have been angrier, but I was depleted, with only so much gas in my tank.

"Did you report it to the police?"

"Yes, they know who he is."

"At least you did the right thing there. Now I have to come and check up on you. Do you see why this lifestyle is dangerous? As flawed as you are, you are the only mother I've got. Are you willing to throw your life away because you want to play room for rent? Jesus, I could have lost you forever."

"John," she said. I did not realize she had left her settee and was now stood over me. "I am sorry for everything. I wouldn't want to be dead, especially not with you being angry with me. You are the softest, purest part of my life."

"Funny, you've always mocked anything soft about me. Be a man, you kept telling me."

She placed both hands on my face.

"I apologise for my own inadequacies, telling you to be tough because I was playing tough. Sometimes you get caught in an act, and you just continue to play the part. The funny thing is, you begin to expect others to play along too."

I concentrated on the familiar scent of tobacco and perfume that emanated from her hands because my head was getting light. I was caught off guard by the woman bending over me.

"I couldn't have done so badly, could I? You still turned out to be a good son—in spite of everything. In spite of me."

"Jesus, you're going to make me cry."

"Maybe it's about time I let you."

28 May 2006

The days after the conversation with my mother, I really didn't know what to do with myself. I had never expected that she would fold so easily. It wasn't that I wanted it to be hard; it was just that her stance over the years had been so solid and unyielding. It was almost a dream. I checked on her as I said I would, but she could take care of herself, as I always found out. She had her ways. Now I just showed up at the house unexpectedly, no calls and no warnings. I laid claim not only on her but on the house too, all of her domain including the gallery.

"So are you going to check on me every day?"

"As many days as I can."

"I am fine, you know. I don't have a husband or a pet, but I'll survive."

She had had to euthanize Tabby some years ago after the cat had become ill.

"I am heading towards the same age that my parents were when they were killed. It was very devastating to lose both my parents when I was thirty-six. I was especially close to my father. He was the best man I ever knew. I could talk to him about anything. He was snatched away, just like that."

"I have never heard you talk about them before, not in this way."

"I don't always want to bring up pain. It was just about then that I started seeking solace in the arms of men. I thought it could be a temporary fix, but sometimes when you meddle with a fix, you get hooked long-term. And my consequence was that I alienated my son and lost two husbands in the process."

"Mom, I am sorry." I touched her cheek as she sometimes touched mine.

She had been remorseful only a night ago, and now I was the one who was apologetic. I had wallowed in my own unhappiness for so long that I had never thought that she might be feeling her own pain too. It was the blindness of being self-centred.

"After more than twenty years, I was glad to talk about it to you. And after the thing with the car, I really had to take stock. I knew you were not necessarily fond of my artists' work, but I thought, *If he comes to the exhibition, maybe we could start to see eye to eye on something.* It would be a beginning of sorts."

"You should have invited me before."

"I never wanted to place you in a position of having to make a decision about something you did not want to do."

I looked around the living room at all the Norval Edwards, the Sandra Spences, and all the others and wondered why I had been so unyielding. It had got me nowhere, and the pieces were still there. They were going nowhere but into the history books on modern art. Maybe steel was a good base for art because it could weather the storm.

"I would have come."

"Probably you would have, but I wanted it to be your free will. You could have come on your own too."

She was right: I could have gone. What would have been so wrong in going? If art is the application of skill to subjects of taste with the objective to perfect workmanship, then what was wrong with what surrounded me? Nothing. They had form and content. It was the mote in the eyes of the skewed viewer and not the object being viewed that was the problem.

It was the end of May, and she had a poster for the Beaches Jazz Festival, which was scheduled in Toronto for the last week in July. I didn't know where she had obtained the colourful advertisement so far in advance of the events, but it told me that she was looking forward to other things. I took note that there would be a Parti Gras in the Distillery District, a street fest at the beach, and another at the main stage at Kew Gardens because I wanted to take her. I also made a mental note to get her some Diana Kraal and some Nora Jones CDs. She could listen to some jazz and blues without too much of the later. She loved Norval Edwards, and I loved the ceramics of Michael Layne. I would get her a vase or a pot, and I would take one of her steel pieces. Either way, it was time to yield.

I felt unburdened and light-headed. Something had been pulled from my grasp, leaving my hands free to hold other things. But what other things? Perhaps hope. Debbie was still away. The festival in St. Lucia would be a week long, but she had decided to stay a second week. Who could blame her for staying two weeks in St. Lucia? The Caribbean was exotic, beautiful, and warm. All I had to do was wait. As long as there was life, there was time.

My aunt invited me to dinner. It seemed strange I was receiving all these invitations around the same time. It was also midweek, but I never said no to Aunt Daphne. I must have assumed that others would be at the dinner because I was surprised to find myself alone with my aunt. Maya wasn't there, and neither was Uncle Mike.

"You really should visit me more often," she said as I kissed her on the cheek.

"Yes, I should, but work takes up so much of my time."

"I hope you are not working too hard. Don't take too many cases home with you. I know it's hard to leave work at work, especially in your field, but you have to have time to think about your own circumstances. Your mind is expansive, but you can only take on so much."

"I know. I try to leave work at work when I leave, but as you say, it's not easy. I cope how I can. I thought there would be other people here."

"No, this dinner is exclusively for you."

"I am flattered, but I don't get it."

"There's nothing to get, really. I just wanted to talk to you."

I assisted her in sharing dinner, wondering about the exclusivity of it and the reason behind her wanting to talk to me. She didn't say anything over dinner, other than the usual dining conversation. We retired afterwards to the sitting room, which was very different from that of my mother's. Hers was filled with photographs of Maya, her husband, and her, along with some pictures of my mother and of me. It was funny how both sisters only had one child. There was no pungent smell of tobacco, only the odour of well-done steak and a tinge of some sort of varnish, maybe furniture polish. There was also the ship Maya mentioned, placed on a stand of some kind. I imagined myself aboard going on a journey; I was making up my mind as to the destination.

"Sometimes people never talk about things that really matter. When they realize that they should talk, it's either too late or it's after things get out of hand. Know what I mean, John?"

"Yea, I see it every day. I see that fault in myself too."

She looked at me closely.

"Do you know why I wanted to become a teacher?" She didn't wait for my response. "I couldn't do anything else. I wanted to shape the lives of young people. I wanted to help. One thing that I have learnt in the profession is that it's not what you know that's important, but how you use the knowledge that you have."

I wasn't sure what she was getting at, but I listened.

"It's the same for our personal lives. Expertise without practicality is a bit futile. Why did you become a therapist?"

"Like you, I wanted to help."

"And have you helped many people with your knowledge of psychology?"

"I think so."

Aunt Daphne brushed invisible lint from her skirt and smiled.

"Have you ever noticed that the people we most want to help with our know-how are often the ones we can't seem to help?"

"Increasingly, these days I'm beginning to see that, but I have no idea what to do about it."

"We've got to give it our best shot, but in the end, we've also got to be practical about what we can and cannot do, and about how long it takes."

I sat facing her, my hands stretched out on the arms of the beige settee. She reminded me of a sage.

"Sounds very simple, but reason and emotions never go hand in hand."

"And I would never want to put them together. I am talking about capabilities, not logics. Specifically, I am talking about your mother. She called me a couple nights ago, after you had left her, and we spoke for a long time. She wanted me to talk to you."

I looked at her and wondered what they had spoken about. What was a conversation between my mother and her sister about her inadequacies like? Their conversation couldn't have been anything like the ones we had had prior to the night of the exhibition.

"Your mother loves you, John."

I nodded.

"She said to me that you and art are the two things that allow her to connect to some beauty and purity."

"I am not that pure anymore. I am just as messed up as the next person."

"You've got to give yourself and your mother time to heal. Don't place a time limit on getting from point *A* to point *B*. And don't think that because you have expertise in your field, you're necessarily going to be able to mend yourself or your mother."

"I don't know whether my mother is ever going to be healed."

"Can you live with that?"

"I'll have to. I love her too, and I am not about to give up on her because she has a problem."

"You're a good son. You always were. Maybe she won't be cured, but she could get to a point in between. Do you remember the butterflies you used to watch?"

"Yes, but that was a long time ago. You know, I don't even have a garden, and I don't have time or carefree days to watch insects go about their days anymore."

"That's too bad, but do you remember why you liked them?"

"Who doesn't like them? They're beautiful. They are also delicate, but I think that's also a part of their beauty."

"Aah, that's like you, your mother, and maybe like most of us. In between the beauty and the fragility, it's not always pretty."

"It was hard to think of my mother being fragile before, but now I can see that she might be."

"It's the fragile who act the toughest. And that fragility is why they act the way they do. The kids in my class who give me the most trouble are the ones who need the most attention."

"My mother needs attention, and I used to believe she didn't need it from me."

"That's where you were wrong; she needs consideration from the people who matter most. The person who matters most to her is you."

It was hard to wrap my head around that. For a very long time, that was the exact opposite of what I had thought.

"I am still not so sure about that."

"Just because she doesn't always show it doesn't mean she doesn't feel it. Have you ever loved anyone but weren't sure how to go about expressing it, for whatever reason?"

I thought of Debbie and wished I were a better man, a man who could show his true emotions.

"I have been there. In fact, I am still there."

"I have the feeling you will get past that. I know a thing or two about grades, and I say you'll make the grade."

"I need some of your confidence; I will take some."

"Everything you need, you have."

My aunt was a teacher responsible for other people's education. I just want to take one piece of what she said and use it, but it's hard to choose one bit because she said so much. Everything she said makes sense, but it all has to be processed. How am I going to reconcile all the things of the past with all the things I know now? And what am I going to do about what I want emotionally and what I am willing to accept?

3 June 2006

Debbie returned from St. Lucia, and that was all that occupied my mind. I now understood what was meant by operating fully within the realm of sensory perception, the place where there is an appeal to a subjective and ultimate goal. I knew she had read my letter because she was very organized and did whatever work she had to do in a timely way. Who knows, she might even have read it before she left for the festival in St. Lucia. One way or the other, she had seen my thoughts. Although I put the ball in her court, I was anxious to see her, and I had to restrain myself from going to her home or office. When this gallantry came over me, I don't know.

She came to me. I heard a knock at the door, and there she was, looking just like yesterday. I had not seen her in months, and I felt like I was about to hyperventilate. I had wanted this, and now that the moment was here, what was I going to do?

"You said you wanted to see me, so I thought I would just drop by."

"Come in," I said as we were still standing by the door. I had no time to prepare.

She looked around. "It smells like paint in here. Wow, the walls are sparkling. You have painted, but the place is still sparse."

"Why bother?" I said, offering her a seat and something to drink, which she accepted.

"So it doesn't bother you that the place is bare?"

"It's clean, and it has most of what I need. Let me show you the bathroom." I led her through the bedroom and showed her the tile job.

"You did this?" The question had incredulity in it because she knew I had never bothered with these things before. But we were we talking about furniture and fixtures, and I wanted to get to the heart of the matter.

"With the help of Paul."

"Impressive. Now all you need is to accessorize."

"I can live with it as is."

"When we lived together, there were many things you could have lived with or without."

The phrase *when we lived together* filled me with all kinds of memories and regrets, but mostly it filled me with wanting her.

"I recognise that and want to rectify it somehow, and that's why I wanted to see you." I launched into the whole sordid affair about my mother because I wanted her to know. It was as if by giving information, I was seeking absolution from her. I was confessing my sins and, by extension, my mother's transgressions.

"Wow, that's quite an account. Couldn't you tell me this before?" She was drawing circles on the glass of fruit punch I had given her.

"The answer to that is quite obvious. No, I couldn't because my manhood was suffering, and telling my wife would only have made it worse. It would have been another castration."

"We both suffered for it. Maybe your faith in yourself as a man would have been restored if you had had a little faith in me."

It was Bob Marley who said, "In the abundance of water, the fool is thirsty." I was that fool, surrounded by smart women and yet sinking and stumbling in stupidity.

"I'm sorry. It was not about faith in you; it was about having faith in myself."

"If I had known what was going on, maybe we would have been able to work it through."

How sad a retrospective can be because in looking back, I see all the roads I could have taken. I see the ways my life could have been different.

"Plus, you can't just lay everything at her feet, you know. You have had a hand in your own decisions about how you were going to live your life and your life with me. I know that we can be receptacles for our parents' belongings, but we can decide to pour out some or all of what they put in. It was up to you to take what you wanted and leave what you didn't."

"I agree with you one hundred percent. It's taken me a while to get to that realization, but I am there."

I looked at Debbie as I imagined a child might look at his mother, wanting something but not having the control to get it.

"I think I am also partially to blame. I saw a kind of remoteness in you, but I still forged along, thinking that it would take care of itself because we loved each other. I didn't investigate what caused it and how it might affect our relationship. To be unaware is not idyllic, not always, anyway."

"I have blamed one woman already for all my problems; I am not going to let you blame yourself."

"It's not about you blaming me; it's about me playing my little part in where we are. It's a sharing arrangement, and it's possible that if I had said let's wait before we made a commitment, you might have faced your foes."

"That's just speculation. If we hadn't gotten married and divorced, I might not have faced up to anything. I might still be going along, calling my mother's name. It's the divorce that pushed me to face my demons. In a sense, you helped me by leaving me."

"It's a roundabout way to give help, especially when I got so hurt in the process."

"I am very sorry about that."

I sank back in the settee, shrinking into the leather because I was repulsed by the hurt I had caused her.

"What's that plant?" She pointed to the potted plant I had bought in the height of winter.

"It's a ponytail palm."

"It's very unusual looking, but I like it, maybe because it doesn't look like every other plant I've seen."

"They also call it "elephant foot" or "bottle palm" because it stores water in its trunk; that's why it looks so engorged. It practically waters itself."

"That's very economical and time saving. But just because it can survive inattention doesn't mean you should ignore it."

"That's one of the reasons I bought it—it feeds itself. But it's the only adornment in this spacious house, so I am constantly drawn to it even though I only have to water it enough to keep the soil from going completely dry. Even though it's indoors, apparently it needs lots of sunlight, so I keep moving it around every day to catch some light. So the lack of attention I had planned is out the window."

"We all need warmth, and sunshine is a good source."

"These palms make flowers but not indoors."

I was happy to be talking about plants and hadn't realized I had a great conversation piece in my living room.

"In any case, I only have one plant, and I was told that the male and female blossoms are on separate plants, so a single plant cannot produce seeds. Even plants are complicated, it seems."

"No, they're not. They are what they are, and the process is what it is, and human reproduction is no different. So, is that the male or female plant?"

"Male, I think."

"Do you think at any time in the near future you are going to get a female plant?"

I didn't think she meant it as a loaded question, but I saw all kinds of connotations in what she said.

"I never really thought about it, but maybe I could do that, and when it's closer to summer, I could put them both outside and see if I get some flowers. I hear they have a yellowish bloom."

"What do you want from me, John?"

There it was. One minute, it was the ponytail palm, and the next, I was right back into the thick of things. The woman in the plant shop had told me something interesting I hadn't known and didn't think about until now. I wanted to tell Debbie, but I had to put my "mantennas" out to sense whether she was ready to hear it. The plant lady had told me that an annual could become a perennial by changing its growing conditions. To me, that spoke to the power of a change of course, and of possibilities that alteration could bring.

"I'm not sure."

I knew I wanted her back, but it wasn't something I was ready to tell her. I couldn't lay everything on her at one time. It just wouldn't have been fair.

"Maybe time to get to know each other in a genuine way this time."

"I don't know, John; I just don't know. I just learned more about you in one night than I did in the two years we were married. It was hard living with someone I didn't know, someone who seemed not to want me to get to know him. Now I don't even know what to do with all this information. I have spent many sleepless nights over this whole thing, and I can finally just be."

I wanted to ask her whether she could just be with me, but I held back. I understood where she was coming from. And I wanted to know who she was. I was willing to wait and compromise until we were on common ground. Maybe this whole business with my mother had made me a narcissist. If I needed healing, she perhaps needed healing too from my follies. Maybe wholeness was just a misplaced desire that I was going after in myself and others without realizing that we are what we are. Could fragmentation and fragility be a part of our completeness?

What I had done for eighteen years was weigh the faults of my mother by putting my hands on the scales. Defining myself by trying to define her. So in the end, a part of me was on the scale too, and I was placed in the balance and found wanting. The funny thing was that she had told me repeatedly that she was who she was. Being her son didn't take away from my own free will. She wasn't perfect, but she didn't make my decisions. At twenty-eight, I could have no more excuses. A man had to take responsibilities for his own actions. Maybe too, I shouldn't judge anything I don't understand. My way of thinking had amounted to a life that I wasn't proud of. But that was my own frailty.

Mom, why did you put that woman on a stand?

Because I want people to look at her and really see her.

Why?

Because she's worthy.

What's worthy?

Oh, my precious six year old, how do I explain this? You said I was like her. Why did you say that?

Because she ... it ... looked perfect, even though it was brown metal.

So you didn't like the stuff that it was made from?

I don't know.

Being worthy means something or someone deserves respect and support, even when that something or someone is flawed. I mean, you might not like the brown metal, but you still like the woman, right?

I guess so, Mom.

5 June 2006

I had two dreams last night, but I did not wake up with the feeling of anxiety I usually had on previous occasions. In one of them, I was washing my hands. It wasn't blood, like Lady Macbeth, but dirt from my garden that I had used to cultivate the seed mix. The last thing I saw before waking was yellow butterflies coming through my window; they were flying all over my room and under the sheets that covered me. They seemed so real, I was really disappointed to wake up and not find them.

I'm not sure why I was washing my hands. After all, my dreams were whatever I imposed on them—figments of my fears and hopes. I wasn't as anguished anymore about the problems that I had let control my life. Maybe I was making a conscious decision of letting go of some of those problems. I would no longer take responsibility for things outside of my control. That was ironic because all I had done was try to control, and in this control I had lost myself. If I gave it up, I could withstand the disorder. I will just breathe and find the strength I had sought in the lack of control.

As for the butterflies, I choose to see them as hope. I am optimistic about a great many things. Debbie has not said yes; she said she didn't know. That is an answer I can live with. If she had said no, I would be done for, and if she had said yes, it would have been too easy. But the ambiguity of *I don't know* gives me an in.

I am thinking of starting a butterfly garden again. I could put my two ponytail palms in the midst of it. It would be a conservation for the insects, but more so for me. The seeds shop on Bloor West will facilitate this undertaking. The girl in the shop said as long as there's a mixture of sun and shade, water, and the right plants, I stand a good chance. It's an ambitious project because I live in a condominium with only a patio. Maybe the butterflies will come, and maybe they won't, but in the end, I wait in hope because they are beautiful to watch.

CPSIA information can be obtained at www.ICGtesting.com
Printed in the USA
LVOW090105300312

275190LV00001B/17/P